Islands of the Black Moon

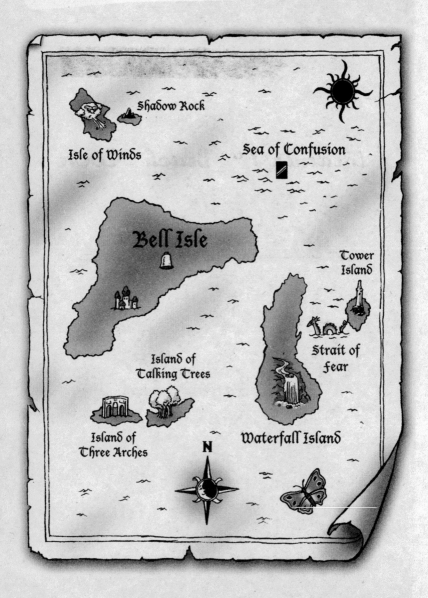

Islands
of the
Black Moon

☾

Erica Farber and
J. R. Sansevere

A Dell Yearling Book

Published by
Dell Yearling
an imprint of
Random House Children's Books
a division of Random House, Inc.
New York

Visit us on the Web! www.randomhouse.com/kids

Educators and librarians, for a variety of teaching tools, visit us at
www.randomhouse.com/teachers

ISBN: 0-440-41706-6

Reprinted by arrangement with Delacorte Press

Printed in the United States of America

June 2004

10 9 8 7 6 5 4 3 2 1

OPM

For Ali
With thanks to Linda
for everything

Prologue

"Once upon a time," my father began, "there was a little boy who dreamed of going to far, faraway lands. Ever since he could remember, he'd wanted to find out what lay just over the horizon, past all the rivers and oceans he knew, including the dangerous Sea of Darkness. When he grew up he became a sailor, and after many long, hard years of learning the ways of the sea, he became captain of his own ship. He made maps and charts and set off on a voyage for the unknown lands on the other side of the world, where sea monsters lurked, ready to gobble up innocent sailors.

"It was a long and difficult journey. Mighty storms tossed the tiny ship up and down, and the winds threatened to tear the very planks of the ship apart.

The sailors grew afraid, but not the captain. All he could think about was reaching that other land just over the horizon, the magical one he'd dreamt of ever since he was a little boy.

"Late one night, the captain woke up suddenly. Something was wrong. The ship was quiet—too quiet. Not a plank groaned, not a sailor snored, not even the sea made the *slap-slap* sounds it always made as the ship moved through the water. The captain ran up on deck. He was all alone. The water's surface was unnaturally still—not a wave rippled even the tiniest bit. But stranger than that, when he raised his eyes to the sky, he saw a huge black moon somehow glowing darker than the night. A shiver went up and down his spine.

"At that moment, a small boat sailed into view. On it was a tall, thin man dressed in a long, tattered robe. He had light hair that hung down his back in a ponytail, but strangest of all were his eyes. They were such a pale shade of blue that they looked almost white. The pale-eyed man stared at the captain with his strange white eyes as he moved his boat closer. Then he raised his hands and held out three glass bottles that glowed like a rainbow in the silvery light of the black moon. And the stranger said, 'Take these bottles far, far from here. Return them to me long years from now, when the time has come.'

"'How will I know when the time has come?' asked the captain.

" 'There will be signs,' answered the pale-eyed man mysteriously.

" 'Where should I take them?' asked the captain.

"The pale-eyed man didn't answer. Instead, he handed the captain a map of a land the captain came to call the Islands of the Black Moon."

"Then what happened?" I asked my father, the same way I did every night. "Did the captain take the magic bottles?"

"Yes, he did," answered my father, the same way he did every night. "And as soon as he did, he heard the most beautiful music. It was the sound of a silver bell ringing. And the man said, 'Listen well, for until the bottles are returned to the place from whence they came, the sound of the silver bell will not be heard again in this land.' "

"I wish I could hear the bell ring," I said with a yawn.

"Maybe one day you will," whispered my father so softly I could barely hear him. "If I'm lucky, on my journey maybe I will too." Then he turned off the light and kissed me good night, the same way he did every night.

"Don't forget my night-light," I said, just like always.

And just like always, he bent and turned it on. He'd given it to me when I was a baby. It was in the shape of a tiny ship, and I couldn't sleep without it.

"Good night. Sleep tight. Don't let the bedbugs bite," said my father. "Remember, I'm leaving to go sailing tomorrow, but I'll be back before you know it."

That was the night of my sixth birthday. When I woke up the next morning, my father was gone. And he never came back.

Chapter 1

Five years later . . .

It all started the day of the science fair. I was really psyched because I was hoping to win first prize. Last year I made a lemon battery by sticking pennies and paper clips into three lemons and hooking up some wires, and then *wham,* those lemons generated enough voltage to light up a very small lightbulb. It was pretty cool. But Peter Peterson, the principal's son and my archrival, beat me. He made singing glasses by putting different amounts of water in a bunch of glasses, rubbing vinegar around the edges, and creating notes. He played the school song, and even though one of his glasses broke, he still won. But this year I was really hoping to beat him.

When I got to school, I went straight to the auditorium where everybody was setting up their projects. It looked like the usual—spiderweb tracings, diagrams of molecules, ant farms. I was so busy checking out the competition, I bumped right into someone.

"Excuse you, da Gama," sneered Peter Peterson, his squinty brown eyes fixed on my shopping bag. "Your project in the bag?" Before I could answer, he continued. "Well, don't get your hopes up, because my project is gonna blow yours away." Then he laughed as if he had said the funniest thing. "For real."

"Whatever," I replied as if I couldn't care less. "If you don't mind, I've got things to do."

I pushed past him to my table, where Sarah Jane Baker was peering glumly at her ant farm.

"What's the matter, Sarah Jane?" I asked.

"Look, Lila," she said, pointing.

Her farm was littered with dead bodies, and the ants had done almost no tunneling. She obviously hadn't realized that red and black ants do not get along. I was trying to think of something to say to cheer her up when Peter Peterson showed up at our table and began setting up. Just my luck.

As I took my project out of the shopping bag, I watched Peterson out of the corner of my eye. Actually, his project did look pretty good. He'd made a volcano out of clay and chicken wire, with a toilet-paper tube stuck in the middle.

"You don't stand a chance against me with that,"

Peterson said, giving my project a nasty grin that revealed the railroad tracks in his mouth.

"We'll see," I said sweetly, as if I couldn't be bothered. "By the way, Peterson, make sure you add the vinegar to the baking soda real slowly. Otherwise you're gonna have a real mess on your hands."

"Shut up, da Gama," Peterson snapped. "I don't need help from some dumb girl."

"You can't say I didn't warn you," I retorted with a shrug. But inside I was fuming. How dare he call me a dumb girl?

"May I have your attention, please?" said Mr. Peterson, the principal, tapping on the microphone. "I can see you've all done some fine work. So let the science fair begin, and may the best man win."

Mrs. Cole, our homeroom teacher, tapped Mr. Peterson on the shoulder and whispered something in his ear.

"I mean," said Mr. Peterson with a huge, phony smile, "may the best person win!"

Like father, like son, I thought, watching as the judges began to thread their way among the tables. I gave my project one last look. It was a telescope I'd made out of two pieces of rolled-up black cardboard, one inside the other. I had fitted a convex lens on one end, the kind of lens that curves outward like the outside of a spoon. I had put another convex lens on the other end. What was tricky was adjusting the lengths of the tubes to make an image come into focus. Next to the telescope was the report I'd written about Galileo Galilei. He's the Italian astronomer who perfected the telescope way back in 1609. He used one concave lens, though, plus a convex one. In case you're interested, concave is the opposite of convex. It's the kind of lens that curves inward like the inside of a spoon. Too bad for old Galileo that he hadn't figured out that two convex lenses work way better.

Before I knew it, Mr. Peterson was at our table examining my telescope, the judges right behind him.

"Good work, Miss da Gama," said Mr. Peterson. "Imagine what it must have been like to be the first man to look into the heavens and find new stars. Amazing!"

"Actually, the most amazing thing Galileo discovered was that the earth was not at the center of the universe, the way everyone else believed it was," I said before I could stop myself. "He found four new planets that were revolving around a bright star, which he figured out was really the planet Jupiter and its four moons. So then he realized that the earth couldn't be the center of the universe, something nobody back then wanted to believe. So he had to appear before the Inquisition, where he was branded a heretic, and then he had to spend the rest of his life under house arrest."

No one said anything for a minute.

"How interesting, Miss da Gama," commented one of the judges, making a note on her pad.

After that, the group moved on to Peter. He might

have had a chance, but he did exactly what I'd warned him not to do. He poured the vinegar into the toilet-paper tube with this big, dramatic flourish instead of dribbling it in nice and slowly. The next thing he knew, the volcano exploded all over the judges. No one likes vinegar much anyway, but when it's all over your clothes, it's pretty disgusting.

When we all gathered to hear the winners, I was thrilled—I won first prize and Peterson came in second.

I was feeling pretty good as I went up onstage to receive my trophy. Peterson was standing right next to me, and before I knew it, he'd shoved his freckly face right next to mine and whispered in my ear, "You only won because they feel sorry for you."

"Wh-what?" I sputtered.

"It's true," continued Peterson under his breath. "My dad told me. Everybody feels bad for you because your dad's dead."

"He is not!" I yelled. "Shut up, Peterson! You're just a sore loser!"

All eyes swiveled toward me, and Mr. Peterson's mouth dropped open in surprise. You can kind of figure what happened next. I had to apologize to Peter Peterson in front of the whole school. On my way home, I tried to look on the bright side. I mean, I had won the science fair, and that was the most important thing, wasn't it?

When I got home, I did my homework first, the way I always do. After that, I went out to the mailbox to get the mail. Since it was almost summer, it was still light out, but I could see Venus shining almost directly above me. A lot of people think Venus is a star because it's so bright, which is why they call it the evening star, but it's really a planet. Anyway, as I stood there in front of the mailbox, I got the strangest feeling, like something weird was going to happen.

When I opened the mailbox, something did. There was a postcard with my name on it, written in spidery, old-fashioned script. It was from my great-aunt Athena, and it was an invitation to spend the summer at Tiger Lily, the falling-apart old hotel where she's lived since long before I was born. I was only ever there once, ages ago. My heart started beating really fast and my stomach did a major flip-flop, but after I read the postcard, I knew I had to go.

> *Dear Lila da Gama,*
> *Now that you have reached the magical age of eleven, it's time for your inheritance. Come to Tiger Lily for the summer.*
> *In haste,*
> *Great-aunt Athena*

No "Hello, how are you?", no "Hope to see you soon." Just that totally strange invitation.

As soon as my mom got home, I told her about the science fair, except the part about apologizing to Peter

Peterson, and I showed her my ribbon. Then I handed her the postcard from Great-aunt Athena.

"You're not going," said my mother in this flat, firm voice that I call her lawyer voice. My mom's a lawyer, by the way.

"Yes, I am," I retorted.

"No, you're not," she said.

"Yes, I am," I insisted, maybe a bit more loudly than I meant to, but Great-aunt Athena is my dad's only living relative. She's also the only one besides me to carry on the da Gama name.

"You're not going, Lila," repeated my mother. "And that's the end of it."

So I said the one thing I knew might make her change her mind. "Mom, I think Dad would have wanted me to go."

My mother didn't say anything for a minute. She started biting her lower lip the way she always did when stuff about my father came up. See, my dad disappeared five years ago, just after my sixth birthday. He's a big-deal physicist, and he'd taken a sabbatical to go on a sailing trip. Most people thought he must be dead, since his boat was never found. But I knew he was alive. I just knew it. And I knew one day he would come back to us. When it first happened, I told my mom that Dad had gone to the Islands of the Black Moon, like in the bedtime story. I was just a little kid then, and she got all teary, and then she sat me down to explain how that was just make-believe and what had happened to Dad was real. So we didn't talk about it much after that.

"I don't know, Lila," my mother finally said with a shake of her head.

Then she proceeded to explain that Great-aunt Athena doesn't know the first thing about children and about how much trouble I would be. Since my mother is a lawyer, she likes facts. She kept going on and on about how Great-aunt Athena lives all alone, how there's no one around for miles in case there's an emergency. Normally, I like facts too—that's why I like science. But I also believe in hunches. A lot of scientific discoveries were made that way. I mean, do you think George Washington Carver had any clue about how terrific a snack he was inventing when he whipped up his first batch of peanut butter? He just had a hunch it was a good idea, the same way I had a hunch about going to Tiger Lily.

Mom sighed this long, heavy sigh, but I could see that her resistance was weakening. See, Mom tries to raise me the way she thinks Dad would have wanted, and every once in a while I have to remind her that I do have Dad's blood and all. So it was decided that night that I could go to Tiger Lily.

Little did I know that getting to Tiger Lily was just the first part of my journey. I would be going much farther than that.

But I'm getting ahead of myself.

Chapter 2

I left for Tiger Lily one hot afternoon at the end of June. I had to take three trains, and the last one was so small it had only two cars—one for the engineer and one for the passengers, which was empty except for me. The train kept stopping and then starting with these shuddering, groaning sounds. Finally, when I was beginning to think I'd never get there, we pulled into the Tiger Lily station.

Right away I spotted the driver Great-aunt Athena had sent. He was driving this old black car—you know, the kind that's long like a couch and has two things that look like fins coming out of the back. The driver held up a sign with my name on it, which I thought was funny since I was the only one getting off at the Tiger Lily stop.

He didn't say much as we drove along, and I didn't either. I was too busy staring at all the trees and wildflowers growing everywhere. There wasn't a house or a store or anything. Just nature every which way you looked. Great-aunt Athena's house sits on top of a big hill. It's three stories high, with a bunch of black wrought-iron balconies and a turret on each side. It looks like a hotel, because that's what it used to be.

The driver set down my suitcase, and before I knew it, he'd driven away. I stared up at the old wooden door, which had a big bronze knocker. My heart began to beat faster in my chest, and the same feeling I'd had by the mailbox the night I got the postcard came rushing back. Something strange was about to happen.

I took a deep breath and knocked. The sound reverberated through the house. I waited, but there was no answer, and I began to wonder if Great-aunt Athena was home. I knocked again, the same strange, fluttering feeling in my stomach.

Finally, I heard a voice coming from somewhere above me.

"Lila!" called a deep, scratchy voice that sounded like the radio when it's between stations. "I'm up here!"

I looked up, squinting in the sun, and there on the roof was Great-aunt Athena. She was wearing a

14

green kimono edged in gold, and it was blowing in the wind so that it ballooned around her like a sail. She was pointing down at me with the same black cane that I remembered from the one time I'd met her so long ago.

I waved and pushed open the door, which creaked on its rusty hinges. I left my suitcase in the dusty front hall.

I took the steps two at a time. Some of them were broken, and lots of them creaked. My mom would have a ton of things to shake her head about if she ever saw this place, but I thought it was cool that Great-aunt Athena had more important things on her mind than a little dust and disrepair. At the far end of the hallway on the third floor, I saw another staircase, smaller and steeper than the others. When I got to the top of that one, I stepped through an arched doorway onto the roof. The sunlight was blinding after the darkness of the house. I had to blink a few times before I could see anything.

When I did, I gasped. The view was amazing. I could see the deep blue of the ocean on one side, with its choppy, white-capped waves. On the other side was a cove, where the water was calm and still because it was sheltered on three sides by rocks. I love the water. I always have. My mom used to joke that I must be part seal or something. I get it from my dad. He started taking me out in his boat and teaching me about sailing practically before I could walk.

"So the last of the da Gamas has come to Tiger Lily," rasped Great-aunt Athena, interrupting my thoughts.

Then she put on her glasses. They were shaped like cat eyes and studded with rhinestones. She looked me up and down as I nodded, the same anticipation making the hairs on the back of my neck prickle. Then she pointed one long red fingernail at me.

"You have the eyes of a true da Gama," she said in that scratchy voice. "Green like the land and blue like the sea. But we shall have to see just how true a da Gama you turn out to be."

Before I could ask her what she meant, Great-aunt Athena took a deep breath. "Do you smell it?" she asked.

I wrinkled my nose. All I could smell was the fishy, salty smell of the ocean.

"You mean the ocean?" I said.

"The sea! The sea!" cried Great-aunt Athena in a booming voice. "The sea is in our blood, you know, because we are da Gamas, descendants of the great explorer Vasco da Gama. He sailed the seas to far-off places where others were afraid to go, looking for new lands, new places, new peoples. He was the first explorer to sail from the West all the way to the East. He saw the signs and followed them. Perhaps you shall see the signs too."

My mother thinks Great-aunt Athena is losing her

memory. What she really means is that she's losing her marbles. You know, that she's cuckoo.

"You may be the one," Great-aunt Athena went on in a whispery voice, more to herself than to me. "The one da Gama to see the signs."

"Signs?" I repeated.

Great-aunt Athena nodded so vigorously her cat-eye glasses fell off her nose. "That's right. Signs. Now come with me. It's time for your inheritance."

So many things were running through my mind, I didn't know what to say. My mouth opened and closed, but no words came out. Great-aunt Athena gave me one last long, appraising look, and then she turned and headed for the door. She led the way, *tap-tap*ping with her cane down all four flights, into a dusty room off the main hallway that had been the library. There were shelves of tattered leather books, a big wooden desk with claw feet in one corner, and an old wooden trunk in the other. Cobwebs covered everything, and the dust was so thick, I felt like I was going to sneeze any second.

Great-aunt Athena didn't say anything at first. She pulled out a small silver key that was hanging on a chain around her neck; then she bent and unlocked the trunk. As she raised the lid, I saw a flash of colors like a rainbow. She pulled two things out and quickly closed the trunk and locked it.

The first thing was a small, blue glass bottle with

an old-fashioned stopper. Staring at the bottle, I shivered, remembering the bedtime story my father used to tell me. But this couldn't be a magic bottle, could it? That was just a story.

The other thing was an old map, which she spread out on the desk. A shaft of sunlight shone into the room just then. It glinted off the bottle and cast sparkles of blue light onto the map. I leaned over the desk and then turned to Great-aunt Athena, who said nothing to prevent me from looking more closely.

The map was yellowed and the corners were curled up. It showed a bunch of islands, and on each island was a picture. One had a waterfall, another one had a tower, one had three arches, another had some trees, another had a rock, and the biggest one had a bell. Between the waterfall island and the tower island was something called the Strait of Fear, which was decorated with choppy lines and a monster in the middle. At the top of the map, there was a strange black circle with black squiggles coming out of it.

"This little bottle holds a powerful secret," whispered Great-aunt Athena.

She twirled the bottle between her fingers. I watched as the blue lights danced across the map. And that was when I saw the butterfly. It wasn't a real butterfly, of course. It was made of the blue sparkles from the bottle. I held my breath, watching as the sparkle butterfly fluttered above the island with the picture of a waterfall on it.

"Did you see that?" I gasped.

"See what?" asked Great-aunt Athena, raising her pencil-thin black eyebrows.

"The butterfly," I answered slowly.

Great-aunt Athena shook her head and stared at me so intently I gulped. When I looked again, the butterfly was gone.

I began, "Was that a si—"

"Shhh!" whispered Great-aunt Athena as she twirled the bottle once more.

The blue lights sparkled across the map again, and this time I saw a star shining above another one of the islands. The one with a tower on it. I remember because it was close to the monster.

But when I blinked, the star was gone.

"I saw another—"

Great-aunt Athena put her fingers to her lips. "They are signs, Lila, to follow as you choose. The secret in the bottle is now yours, for you are the first da Gama who has ever seen the signs."

"You mean you never saw the . . . uh . . . signs?" I asked with a shiver.

Great-aunt Athena shook her head. "No, I did not," she said softly. "And neither did your father, nor my mother, nor her mother's father, nor any da Gama on back for generations and generations." She handed me the bottle. "Do not open it until you are ready, for there may be no turning back once you begin."

I turned the bottle upside down and sideways. I

held it up and peered into its murky blue depths. Finally, I studied the small stopper. So this little blue bottle was my inheritance? What was in there that could be so powerful?

"You are the last of the da Gamas," whispered Great-aunt Athena in a solemn voice. "It could be a gift. It could be a curse."

Chapter 3

I asked Great-aunt Athena a ton of questions about the bottle, but she couldn't—or wouldn't—tell me anything more about it. After dinner, I went upstairs to unpack. I put my clothes in an old wooden wardrobe that sat in a corner. Then I put my picture of my dad on the table beside the bed. And finally, I plugged in my old ship night-light. Like I said, I really can't sleep without it.

"I trust you have everything you need for the night," said Great-aunt Athena, poking her head into my room. "I take a sleeping potion, you know, so once I'm asleep I never wake up before morning." She kissed me quickly on the cheek. "Now good night, my dear. Sleep tight. Don't let the bedbugs bite."

"That's what my dad used to say to me," I blurted out in surprise.

Great-aunt Athena just smiled, and before I could ask her anything else, she disappeared into her bedroom and closed the door.

It was really hot that night, and it was too early to sleep. It was still light outside. I tossed and turned, but I couldn't relax. My eyes kept going to the little blue bottle, watching as the glass sparkled in the glow from the night-light. I decided to go down to the cove to cool off. Great-aunt Athena had told me I was free to roam, so I figured that was okay. I slipped out of bed, pulled on shorts and a T-shirt, stuck the bottle in my pocket, and headed downstairs.

Outside I made my way through tall evergreens and drooping willow trees. Tiger lillies were growing wild everywhere. I guess that's how Tiger Lily got its name. Finally, I reached the dock. At the end, I saw a wooden raft that wasn't attached to the dock but anchored on the sandy bottom, so I took off my sneakers and headed out to it. I sat on the raft's edge and dangled my feet in the dark, still water, listening to the locusts buzzing in the trees and the bullfrogs croaking. It must have been close to nine o'clock, because the sun was finally setting and the first stars twinkled in the sky. I watched the pale pink and red glow as it began to disappear into the water, and I watched the lights from Great-aunt Athena's house up on the hill.

I reached into my pocket and pulled out the blue

bottle. The glass felt smooth and cool. I shook it, but it made no sound. It was probably empty.

My fingers itched to open it.

"Why not?" I said aloud.

I was about to pull out the stopper when Great-aunt Athena's words of warning ran through my mind.

This little bottle holds a powerful secret. . . . Do not open it until you are ready.

Ready for what? I wondered. I would never know unless I opened the bottle. So, before I lost my nerve, I took a deep breath and slowly pulled out the stopper. My heart was pounding in my chest and I was staring like a genie was going to pop out or something. But you know what? Nothing happened. The bottle was empty. With a sigh, I put the stopper back in and put the bottle in my pocket. Maybe my mom was right and Great-aunt Athena really was batty. I lay down on the raft and closed my eyes.

Suddenly, the wind began to blow. I could hear it whooshing through the trees, making the branches creak and snap. I sat up as lightning streaked across the black sky. A clap of thunder crashed right over my head. The wind blew even harder, and waves rocked the raft up and down.

I tried to get back to the dock, but I couldn't even stand up.

Then a hole opened in the air, almost like a door, and through the door I could see sunlight. All around the door was darkness, but through the door was light. It seemed to be coming from another place. From another world.

The raft broke loose from its anchor with a lurch. It began to spin around wildly, faster and faster and faster. I tried to hold on, but I lost my grip. The wind knocked me right off the raft, but I didn't fall into the water. I fell through that hole in the air, through the door of light.

I fell into another world.

When I turned back, the door was gone and Tiger Lily was gone, too.

I looked around, trying to stay calm, but it's hard to be calm when you suddenly find yourself alone in a strange world. I was standing on a beach of the whitest sand I have ever seen. The blue bottle was lying on the sand, so I picked it up and put it in my pocket. The sand was so fine and soft it felt like powder between my toes. The water was a rich turquoise that glittered in the bright, hot sunlight. Behind me there were palm trees. A whole jungle of them.

Now what? I wondered, staring from the dunes at one end of the beach to the piles of rocks at the other. I had no time to be scared before a shadow fell over me. When I looked up I saw a big green bird, with a hooked beak and round blue eyes, flying above me. The bird disappeared into the jungle and I heard a horrible sound, like a wolf howling and a snake hissing at the same time. It seemed to be coming from the direction of the dunes.

Seconds later, giant lobsters, covered in shiny red armor, appeared. Each one was as big as a couch and had three sharp claws, two in front for pinching and one on top to hold a dangling eyeball. The hideous creatures slid through the sand on their bellies like giant armored worms.

They were coming for me!

I ran toward the palm-tree jungle, desperate for a place to hide. I stumbled through the strange, viney plants that were growing everywhere. Suddenly, my foot got caught on something and I tripped. Before I knew it, I was yanked up into the air.

I screamed.

I was hanging upside down from a palm tree with my foot caught in some kind of trap. I pulled and pushed, but the noose around my foot only got tighter. And those horrible creatures were hissing and howling and snapping their claws like they knew I couldn't get away.

It looked like I was a goner.

Chapter 4

"Ka-noo-choo-weeeeeee!"

A boy swung out of the trees and landed on the sand in front of the creatures. They stopped dead in their tracks.

"Go!" he yelled, waving a stick high in the air. "She's mine! I caught her fair and square!"

The creatures lowered their eyeballs and slithered away as fast as they could, hissing and howling as they went.

The boy laughed. "Claw-clops!" he said. "If they could see themselves, they would be scared to death."

He sauntered over to me. He looked funny, but that might have been because I was still hanging upside down. He was dressed in ragged clothes, and he had a blue cloth tied around his head.

He stared at me without a word, a big grin on his face.

"Let me down!" I ordered.

"I ain't going to let you down unless you've got something to trade," said the boy.

"Trade?" I exclaimed.

"That's right," said the boy. "And I'm only gonna do it if you've got something I want."

"I haven't got anything to trade," I sputtered. "You let me down right this minute, whoever you are. Where I come from, people don't catch each other in traps."

The boy just shrugged and turned away.

"Hey, you, where do you think you're going?" I yelled.

The boy turned and grinned at me again. "My name is Deco," he said. "And if you don't got nothing to trade, then I'll just leave you here for the claw-clops. It don't matter to me."

"You can't do that!" I yelled.

But the boy just walked away, swinging his stick and whistling.

Suddenly, I remembered the blue bottle. I hoped I hadn't lost it. I felt in my pocket and gave a sigh of relief as my fingers closed around the smooth, cold shape. I pulled it out.

"Wait!" I called, holding out the bottle. "I do have something."

27

Deco turned slowly and looked up at the bottle. The blue glass glinted in the sunlight.

"Give it to me!" he said. "Then I'll let you down."

"No, let me down first," I retorted. "Then I'll give it to you."

Deco stared at me, so I stared back. Everything looked weird from my upside-down position.

"Okay," Deco said slowly. "But you better not try anything. Or I'll hang you up in the tree again and then the claw-clops can have you for dinner. Swear?"

"I swear," I said.

"Put your hand on your heart and let me see your fingers ain't crossed," continued Deco, watching me closely.

Quickly, I uncrossed my fingers. "I swear," I said again as I crossed my toes.

Deco pulled a small wooden thing that looked like a boomerang from his belt. Then he started walking away again.

"Hey, wait!" I cried. "I promised. Remember?"

Deco turned then, and with one smooth motion he hurled the boomerang at me. The next thing I knew, I was lying on the ground, coiled up in rope.

"I'm pretty good with a boomerang, huh?" he said with a mischievous twinkle in his brown eyes. "Now give me the bottle."

Two can play at this game, I thought as I watched Deco putting the boomerang back in his belt. I didn't waste another moment. I wiggled out of the rope and ran as fast as I could, right into the jungle. The vines were so thick they were like a green curtain. I used my hands to push my way through them, but it was tough going. Ahead, I could hear running water, but I couldn't see it.

Finally, I got through. And there, behind the vines, I saw what was making the sound—a waterfall.

Suddenly, I was grabbed from behind. Before I fell, I threw the bottle as hard as I could. It landed somewhere in the tangle of vines on the other side of the waterfall.

"The bottle's mine!" burst out Deco. "You swore."

"I crossed my toes, so the swear doesn't count," I hissed between clenched teeth.

I tried to get up, but Deco was holding my legs.

"No one can cross their toes," he scoffed.

"I can," I said. "My second toe is bigger than my big toe. See?" I wiggled my toes and showed him. "It happens to be a sign of intelligence, by the way."

Then, while he was looking at my toes, I kicked him in the stomach. He gasped and let go of me. I jumped to my feet, staring across the waterfall toward the tangle of green viney plants where I'd thrown the bottle. I saw a flash of blue glass. It had to be the bottle.

"Owww," moaned Deco, clutching his stomach.

I looked from him to the bottle and then back to him again. "Are you okay?" I finally asked, leaning over him. "I didn't mean to kick you so hard, but—"

Before I knew it, he'd jumped up and tackled me.

"You faker!" I screamed as we both rolled to the ground.

Suddenly, Deco let go of me. He clapped his hand over my mouth and pulled me down behind a large tangle of vines. His head was cocked to one side like he was listening to something, and he had a really scared look on his face.

"Shhh!" he whispered.

Chapter 5

I listened really hard and finally heard an eerie swishing sound, almost like the wind. The next thing I knew, the ground began to shake. Deco and I both peeked through the vines toward the beach. A platoon of men on horses were riding toward us, dressed in red-and-black armor, with gleaming silver swords by their sides. The man in front wore a red turban, and the rest all wore white ones, decorated with feathers. As they rode, the feathers blew in the wind, making the swishing sound. Other than that noise, there was silence. None of the horses whinnied even once.

But stranger still were the men's faces. As they rode closer, I saw that they didn't have human heads but the orange-and-black-striped heads of tigers.

When they got to the edge of the jungle, they stopped. They were only a stone's throw from where we were hiding behind the vine curtain. They scanned the area with their tiger eyes. One of them pointed to our footprints in the sand.

"Don't move!" whispered Deco. "It's the manticores!"

"Who?" I whispered back, staring at the tiger soldiers in horror.

"The sultan's army!" Deco murmured, putting his finger to his lips.

I sat really still, holding my breath. Sweat beaded on my forehead and dripped down my nose as I stared at those scary manticores. One of them was holding a flag, with a picture of a black circle with black squiggles coming out of it. It looked very familiar, but before I could figure out why, the manticore with the red turban dismounted. The big green bird I'd seen before swooped in front of him and cawed once, staring into the jungle with its round blue eyes.

The bird's eyes locked onto mine.

I looked at the bottle, still sitting in the vines across the waterfall.

"Don't even think about it," Deco ordered, glancing at me out of the corner of his eye. "They're too fast. You'll never make it."

"I'm fast too," I said.

I jumped to my feet, but before I'd taken more than three steps, I heard that swishing sound. I stopped dead in my tracks. The leader was standing right in front of me. It was almost like he'd beamed himself there.

He stepped closer and bared his razor-sharp tiger fangs. Then he pointed his sword at me, the long blade glinting in the sunlight.

"Don't move!" shouted Deco. "Or you'll be history."

I gulped as I stared into his scary yellow tiger eyes.

"In the name of the sultan, surrender the blue bottle," the leader commanded.

And that was when the blue butterfly came. It fluttered toward me and landed on my hand. Seconds later a whole swarm of butterflies appeared, their colorful wings sparkling in the sunlight, like a rainbow. A woman dressed in a long, shimmering robe appeared in the middle of them. As I stared at her, I saw why her robe was shimmering—she was covered with butterflies.

The butterfly woman went right up to the leader. "Tell the sultan that this girl is not the one who has brought back the bottles," said the butterfly woman in a gentle, musical voice. "The See-It-All made a mistake."

"The See-It-All?" I repeated.

"The bird," Deco whispered, moving to stand next to me.

I remembered that I'd seen the green bird on the beach when I first arrived.

"But the See-It-All told us she has come with the blue bottle," said the leader with a nod of his red turban.

The butterfly woman laughed, then stared into his yellow tiger eyes. Colored lights shot out of her eyes, bright as fireworks. The manticore's yellow eyes glazed over as he stared into the woman's multicolored ones.

"There is no girl here," she crooned in her singsong voice. "You have been misinformed. See for yourself."

The leader turned his gaze to me, but it was like I really wasn't there. His yellow eyes were blank. They looked right through me.

"I see," he said, bowing before the butterfly woman. "There has been a mistake."

The next thing I knew, he was gone. He must have moved with that lightning speed back to the beach, faster than I could see him go.

The butterfly woman smiled at me as the butterflies fluttered in a multicolored cloud all around her.

"I am Ione," she intoned in her musical voice. "I have been waiting for you."

Chapter 6

Ione smiled at me again, a special smile, like the two of us shared a secret. She looked into my eyes with her magical ones. First they were blue like the sky, then golden like the sun, then silver like the moon, then green like emeralds. They were the most beautiful eyes I had ever seen, and I couldn't look away from them.

"You have brought the blue bottle," crooned Ione in her lullaby voice. Her words mingled with the gentle fluttering of the butterflies.

"Well," I began, "I . . . kind of . . ."

"I have been waiting for that bottle for a long time," she continued, her now silver, now blue, now gold, now green eyes never leaving my face. "Ever since the Keeper gave it to the sea captain. The captain promised that one day someone would bring it back."

My heart began to beat faster. Sea captain just like the captain in the bedtime story? She had to mean Vasco da Gama, my ancestor, didn't she? I was about to run and get the bottle when her eyes flashed again, a sparkle of lights like firecrackers. It woke me from my trance. How did I know I wasn't just falling under another one of Ione's spells? Until I had cold, hard, scientific proof that I was supposed to give her the bottle, it suddenly didn't seem like such a good idea at all.

So I took a deep breath and looked away from those glittering eyes. And I made sure not to glance at the falls, where the bottle lay in the vines, just feet from where Ione stood staring at me.

"Give me what I wish," crooned Ione. "Give me the blue bottle, fashioned of the stuff of dreams, filled with a power I alone understand."

It took every ounce of self-control I possessed not to look at Ione, or even worse, at the bottle.

"Look at me," chanted Ione, stepping closer. "Look into my eyes and do as I command."

I gritted my teeth, but it was no good. I felt myself turning toward the source of that magical voice.

"Is the bottle valuable?" Deco suddenly asked, breaking the spell.

"Priceless," hissed Ione with a sigh of annoyance.

"Well, she did have the bottle," said Deco slowly, "but then she gave it to me."

"Is this true?" Ione asked me, her eyes narrowing. "Did you give this boy the blue bottle?"

"Not exactly," I replied.

"You know you did when I saved you from the claw-clops," put in Deco. "We made a deal."

I didn't say anything. I guess Deco didn't believe me about my toes being crossed.

I watched as Ione moved toward Deco, her feet never seeming to touch the ground. Then she gazed into his eyes and began to speak to him in the same lullaby voice she had used on me.

"So are you the one who has the blue bottle?" Ione floated even closer to Deco, smiling her special smile at him. "Tell me where it is, boy, and you shall be a hero."

"Don't tell her!" I shouted.

It was too late. Deco's eyes had already darted across the falls to the green viney plants. Ione followed his gaze, and a small smile of triumph appeared on her cold, beautiful face. "The blue bottle," she whispered to herself. "Finally."

I had to get to the bottle before she did. Deco must have been thinking the same thing, because we both made a run for it. Together we splashed through the water to the other side of the falls, but just as we reached the bottle, it began to move. It was like the vines had invisible hands that were passing the bottle along. The bottle moved away from us faster and faster. We chased it, but Ione, who hadn't moved an inch, was holding the bottle in her own hands before we could even come close.

Deco and I froze.

"Such a beautiful bottle," she murmured, holding it up to the light.

"It's mine," I yelled. "And you know it."

I reached for it, but the vines coiled around my body like snakes, holding me back so that I couldn't move.

"Let us go!" Deco yelled. "Make the crawlers let us go."

Ione wasn't about to set us free. With a toss of her long, dark hair, she laughed and turned to walk away.

"Wait!" I cried.

I couldn't let her take the bottle, since I was pretty sure the man she'd called the Keeper was the man in my father's bedtime story who had given the three bottles to the captain. And I was positive neither of them would have wanted me to hand the blue bottle over to a sorceress. Plus, I figured that since the blue bottle was what had brought me here, it might be the only way I'd ever get back to Tiger Lily.

"What can I do to get the bottle back?" I asked.

"Why should I let you do anything?" she whispered, smiling so that her eyes flashed. "The bottle is mine now."

"I'll do anything." I made sure not to look into those shimmering, changing eyes of hers.

I felt Ione study me for a long minute. "Then bring

me a star," she said slowly. She smiled then, as if she had a secret.

"A star!" I repeated in shock. "But that's impossible."

She laughed again. "Of course," she said. "If you can do that, I will give you back the blue bottle. But if you cannot, not only do I keep the bottle, but you must agree to do what I say."

"If I bring you a star," I continued desperately, "do you swear you'll give me the bottle?"

"I give you my word," intoned Ione solemnly.

"How do I know I can trust you?" I asked.

"You can," Deco chimed in. "A sorceress never breaks her word. If she did, she would lose her power."

Ione laughed once more, the sound echoing in the stillness. Then she disappeared into the jungle, the butterflies shimmering all around her like a cloud. I looked at Deco and he looked at me, the same question in his eyes and mine.

How in the world was I ever going to bring her a star?

Chapter 7

"There are no stars on these islands," Deco announced matter-of-factly. "I should know. I've traveled to most of 'em."

I began to pace and twirl a strand of hair around one finger, the way I always do when I'm thinking. "A star," I said again.

Deco cocked one eyebrow at me before he began to polish his boomerang with the tattered end of his shirt. I'd seen a star recently, but where? Back at Tiger Lily the night on the dock. But that wasn't what was tickling my memory.

"There's only one place I can think of where there's stars," continued Deco. "And that's the sky."

"The map!" I exclaimed, jumping up and down. "That's where I saw a star!"

"Huh?" Deco looked at me like I was crazy.

"My great-aunt Athena showed me a map," I began excitedly. "It must have been a map of these islands, because it had the same black circle the manticores had on their flag. Anyway, there was an island with a tower on it and I saw a sign—a star shining on top of that island with the tower."

"What are you talking about?" asked Deco, twirling his boomerang.

"I need a boat," I said quickly.

"What are you going to do?" countered Deco. "Sail to the sky and bring her back a star?"

"This is no time for jokes," I said. "Do you have a boat or don't you?"

Deco straightened his shoulders proudly. "I've got a sailboat."

"See, the blue bottle made these strange sparkles and I saw a star shining on top of that island with the tower," I explained. "So, if we go to that Tower Island, I figure maybe we'll find a star there. I found butterflies on this island after the blue bottle sparkled a butterfly over Waterfall Island on the map. If the butterfly was a sign then the star probably is, too. The question is—where is Tower Island?"

I closed my eyes and tried as hard as I could to remember the map. I could see Waterfall Island, where we were now. I could see Tower Island, where we wanted to go. I picked up a stick and drew a map in the sand. "There!" I exclaimed. "Tower Island is east of us."

In silence Deco studied the map I had drawn. Finally, he pointed to the space between the two islands and said, "We can't go there. That place is cursed."

"What?" I burst out. "Have you ever been there? Do you even know where it is?"

"No, I ain't been there," said Deco slowly. "But there's this sea monster that lives there."

"What are you talking about?" I asked, trying hard not to lose my temper.

"The Strait of Fear," said Deco slowly, pointing again to the spot in the sand between the two islands. "It's where the sea monster lives. And when it breathes, the water goes in crazy circles. If a boat gets stuck in one of those circles, the sea monster swallows it."

"Are you kidding?" I exclaimed, staring at Deco like he had just sprouted a second head. "There's no such thing as sea monsters." Of course, where I came from there were no talking tiger men or See-It-All birds either, but I decided to ignore that fact.

"Everybody knows there are sea monsters," retorted Deco.

"I think you're just scared," I said.

"I'm not scared," replied Deco. "But I'm not stupid, neither."

I let that one go. "Look, if you're so afraid, I'll just

go by myself," I said. "I know how to sail. My dad taught me when I was little."

"I'm not scared," he said again.

"Right," I said, raising one eyebrow. No way did I believe that. "Just take me to the boat, okay? And I'll be on my way."

Deco put his boomerang back in his belt. Then, without a word, he led the way down the beach, toward the rocks. There was an old wooden raft hidden behind the rocks. Hanging from a pole sticking up out of it was a raggedy piece of cloth. One old splintered wooden paddle sat on the deck.

"You call that a boat?" I burst out before I could stop myself. "It looks like a beat-up old raft to me."

"It's a sailboat," said Deco, eyeing his raft with pride. "And it's taken me lots of places."

"Except to the island where I want to go," I pointed out.

"Are you going to stand here and talk all day?" said Deco. "Or do you want to go? It's a long way."

With that, he grabbed one end of the raft, so I grabbed the other. We dragged it across the sand into the water.

"Get on," ordered Deco.

I hopped onto the raft, holding the paddle, while Deco walked behind me and pushed the raft through the waves. When we got past the white water, he jumped on.

"You're coming?" I said in surprise.

"Of course," he answered. "If I didn't, I doubt I'd see my boat again."

"Very funny," I said, "but I happen to be a pretty good sailor."

"We'll see," said Deco as we headed out into the open sea. "We'll take turns paddling."

The sun had passed the midday point and was heading slowly toward the west.

"Go that way," I said, pointing away from the sun. "The island's to the east of us, remember?"

Deco gripped the raggedy sail and turned it. After he had paddled for a while, it was my turn. The wind had picked up, so he turned the sail to catch the breeze.

"So where do you live?" I asked, partly just to be friendly and partly because I figured the more I knew about the islands, the better.

"Here and there," Deco answered vaguely.

"What do you mean?"

"Just what I said," he answered.

"Well, do you live on Waterfall Island?"

"Course not," replied Deco, looking at me like I was crazy. "Nobody lives there. Everybody lives on Bell Isle."

"Bell Isle?"

Deco nodded. "That's where the sultan's palace is."

"So that's where your parents are?"

Deco looked away. "I don't have parents. I take care of myself, like most of the kids."

"Oh." I know what it's like to not have a dad—but I couldn't imagine not having a mom either.

"What's the sultan's palace like?" I asked after a minute.

Deco frowned. "Well, nobody's ever been in there. Not really. I mean, I know somebody who made it past one gate, but then the manticores got him and they threw him in the dungeon."

"What kind of a ruler would throw someone in jail for something little like that?"

Deco shrugged. "I don't know. Nobody really knows anything about the sultan because nobody's ever seen him. He never leaves his palace. Some people say he's under a spell."

"What kind of spell?"

"The kind of spell that makes it so you can walk and talk and stuff but you're not really there."

"I don't believe in magic spells," I said. "There's probably some rational explanation for the sultan's behavior. Maybe he's sick or something."

"Maybe," said Deco.

"What's Bell Isle like?" I asked.

Deco shrugged. "It's got lots of twisty streets. The houses are small and falling apart. Smells kind of like garbage, I guess."

"Why's it called Bell Isle?"

" 'Cause there's a big silver bell in an old stone tower by the sultan's palace. People say it used to ring and make the most beautiful music, back in the old days when people were happy and stuff. Supposedly, one day the bell will ring, and when it does, there'll be happiness again. Pretty silly, huh?"

I didn't say anything as the words of my father's bedtime story came rushing back. I shivered in the hot sunlight.

"What will make it ring?" I asked, holding my breath.

Deco scratched his head. "I forget," he said. "Or maybe I never knew. What's it matter, anyway? It ain't rung for years and years."

We didn't say much after that, just took turns paddling. The wind had died down, so the whole afternoon went by before we got to the narrow channel I remembered from the map—the Strait of Fear. As we began to paddle across it, I spotted the other island. It rose out of the water like a mountain in the middle of the sea. Poking out of the trees at the top was a tower.

I was just about to point to the tower when waves started to crash against the raft. The raft began to spin around and around in circles.

"It's the sea monster!" shouted Deco over the roar of the waves. "We're doomed!"

"It's not a monster!" I shouted back. "It's a whirlpool."

We spun faster and faster. A wave hit me in the

face. Water filled my mouth and went up my nose. I struggled to catch my breath.

"I told you this place was cursed!" cried Deco.

I didn't say anything. I couldn't. I just held on tight so I wouldn't be thrown overboard into the whirlpool and be sucked under. Maybe Deco was right.

Deco turned the sail, but when it caught the wind it only made us go in faster circles. He tried to turn it again, but he lost his grip and fell into the swirling water.

"Deco!" I cried.

But his head disappeared beneath the waves.

"Deco!" I cried again.

His head bobbed up. I leaned down and stuck the paddle into the water.

"Grab it!" I shouted.

Deco reached for the paddle, but just as he was about to grab it, a wave rolled over both of us. I struggled to stay on the raft. Deco kept bobbing up and down, but finally, he grasped the paddle, and I pulled on it as hard as I could. His chest landed on the raft first. Then I managed to pull the rest of him aboard. The problem was, we were still spinning around and around. I had to do something or we were both going to drown.

If only we had a rudder, I thought. And that gave me an idea. I inched my way to the edge of the raft farthest from the sail, and I shoved the paddle into the swirling water.

"Turn the sail to the left!" I shouted.

Deco held on to the sail and pulled with all his might. I knelt down and pushed the paddle into the swirling water, trying to turn it into a rudder. But the current was so strong, I kept almost losing my grip. It looked like I had no other choice. Slowly, I lay belly down and inched my way to the edge of the heaving raft. Then I thrust the paddle into the water as hard as I could and held on to it with every ounce of strength I possessed. Finally, the raft swung around, the sail caught the wind, and we sailed out of the whirlpool to the island.

As I looked back at the swirling water, Deco said, "Wow! How'd you do that?"

"I told you I'm a good sailor," I replied.

After that, it didn't take long to reach the island. Tower Island didn't have a sandy beach for us to land on, though. It had tall stone cliffs, which rose steeply before us. The water there was flat like a sheet of glass. We paddled the raft to a rock and tied it up with a raggedy piece of string Deco pulled out of his pocket. It was really quiet, and there didn't seem to be anybody around. And it was getting dark.

I looked up and saw the strangest thing. There was an almost full moon in the sky, but it didn't look like any moon I had ever seen before. It was pitch black instead of white, blacker than the night.

"Why is the moon black?" I asked.

"Because it's a black moon," answered Deco, like

my question was the silliest thing he'd ever heard. "Don't they have black moons where you come from?"

I shook my head. We didn't have claw-clops or manticores or sorceresses like Ione, either. But I didn't say that.

"Let's try up there," I said instead, pointing to what looked like some steps in the side of the rock.

By the time we got to the top of the steps, it was really dark. The only thing I could see was a tiny flickering light high above us.

"Look!" I cried, pointing.

As we drew closer, I saw that the light was coming from a candle in a window. The window was at the top of the tower I had seen from the raft. The door to the tower had strange carvings all around it, almost like zodiac signs. I banged on the door with the old, rusty knocker. We waited a few minutes, but no one came.

I stepped back to look up at the window again. The light was gone.

"Someone's up there," I said. "I just know it."

Without a word, Deco pushed on the door, and it slowly creaked open. Then the two of us stepped inside, and the door slammed behind us.

We were in total darkness.

Chapter 8

"Now what?" Deco whispered.

"We have to find the stairs," I whispered back.

"Why?"

"To get to the top where the light was. I'm sure there's somebody up there who can help us."

It was so dark I couldn't even see my hand when I held it up in front of my face. I got down on all fours and crawled forward, feeling around. Finally, I felt something hard and smooth. It was a step.

"Over here!" I said.

The two of us crawled slowly up the stairs.

"Twenty-eight . . . twenty-nine . . . ," I counted as the steps curved around and around.

There was a loud thud above our heads. We both stopped.

"I told you there was somebody up there," I said, trying to sound more confident than I felt.

"Or some*thing*," put in Deco.

We kept climbing and I kept counting as we went. Seventy-three . . . seventy-four . . . Finally, the darkness began to lighten. When I reached one hundred and one, the steps stopped. We were at the top.

I blinked, staring in surprise. We were in a small, round room with windows all around it that allowed the silvery light of the black moon to filter in. Long metal tubes, some thick and some thin, pointed out the windows. In the center of the room stood a scarred and scratched wooden table covered with pieces of glass of different shapes and sizes. There were mirrors and tools and sheets of paper with marks all over them.

I walked over to one of the shorter tubes and studied it carefully. There were two lenses, one on each end.

"What is it?" asked Deco.

"An old telescope," I told him.

"Huh?" said Deco.

"You know, a telescope. Something you look through to study the sky. I have one at home." And that's when it hit me—I knew exactly how I was going to bring Ione a star.

Before I could tell Deco, I heard a creaking sound. I

whirled around just as a trapdoor in the floor began to open. Deco jumped back.

Out crawled an old man with long white hair. He was wearing a tattered blue robe with strange pictures on it that matched the carvings on the door.

"You have studied the sky?" the old man asked me, his bushy eyebrows raised in surprise. "But it is forbidden."

"Not where I come from," I answered. "Why would anybody forbid studying the sky?"

"All pursuits of knowledge are banned on the islands," said the old man in a heavy voice.

"But why?"

"Because that's the way it is," put in Deco.

"It has been this way for half a century," said the old man with a sigh. "Ever since Vulnyx had the sultan put under a spell and ordered the army to destroy all books and all scientific equipment."

"Who's Vulnyx?" I asked.

Deco's eyes widened. "They say he's some kind of monster, with big black wings and bloodred eyes. He can suck your blood or kill you with one look."

The old man shook his head. "I don't know about that, but I do know that he had all my fellow scientists and inventors, astronomers and doctors locked up in a dungeon at the Isle of Winds. I alone managed to escape. I felt it was my duty to continue my colleagues' work in all areas of science. As a result, I've mapped the human body, invented a compass to tell direction at sea, built military catapults with gears and pulleys, discovered how to use a pendulum to make a clock that tells the time down to the minute, and much more."

"Wow!" I exclaimed, studying the old man with respect. "You did all that in fifty years?"

"That's right," answered the old man with a sigh. "And now I've just begun my study of the heavens. So tell me, how do you study the stars?"

"By looking at them through a telescope," I said. "In fact, I built one myself. Not nearly as nice as these. It was only made of cardboard, but I won first prize in the science fair."

The old man frowned. "Telescope? Don't you mean spyglass?"

"We call them telescopes," I said.

"I see," remarked the old man. "Well, it doesn't matter what you call them. No matter what I do to make them work better, the stars are just blurs of light. The secrets of the sky remain a mystery to me."

"Can I take a look?" I asked.

The old man nodded.

I looked into the short, dark metal spyglass, turning it first one way and then another. I could see some stars.

"This one works," I said.

"Yes, but not well enough for me to see the mountains and valleys of the moon," replied the old man.

I could see what he meant. I peeked into another spyglass. This one was very long and thin. When I looked through it, all I could make out was a blurry mass of light. I moved on to the next one, which was very short. When I looked through it, everything was even blurrier.

"Do you mind if I take off the eyepiece lens?" I asked.

The old man just looked at me and shrugged. I examined the eyepiece.

"Oh, no," I said. "This lens is concave. It'll work way better if its convex."

"Concave? Convex?" the old man frowned. "Are these sorcerer's words?"

"No," I answered. "Just scientific."

Then I turned the telescope around to study the lens on the other end. "This lens is right. It's convex, just like it's supposed to be."

The old man looked at me like I was crazy.

"See, a concave lens is one that's thicker at the edges than it is in the middle." I held up the eyepiece. "A convex lens is just the opposite. It's thicker in the middle than it is at the edges." I pointed to the lens on the end of the telescope.

"I see," murmured the old man. But I could tell that he didn't really see what I meant at all.

"What you need to see the stars better is two convex lenses. The first one you use for the eyepiece. You know, the lens that you look through. That's the one that does the magnifying."

I stopped to let what I had said sink in.

"The second one you put on the other end, just the way you have it. That lens bends light rays from the object that you're looking at. It's the one that brings what you're looking at into the telescope so you can see it. In this case, the stars."

I stopped again, watching him think it over.

"So after that lens brings the stars into the telescope, then the eyepiece makes them look bigger. Now, where are your convex lenses?"

"Lenses that are thicker in the middle than at the edges?" he asked, frowning.

"Exactly," I replied.

"I have many lenses like that there on the table."

"Well, once you find one that fits, you'll be able to see all kinds of stuff—even mountains and valleys on the moon."

I didn't want to tell him that we call them craters. Or that we'd sent men to the moon a bunch of times. I had a feeling it would blow his mind.

The old man tried one convex lens after another until he found one that fit. Finally, he stood back, a big smile on his face.

"Amazing!" he remarked. "Thank you, my young friend! I can never repay you."

"Well, actually you can," I said. "Do you think I could have one of your tele—I mean spyglasses? I don't want it for myself. See, there's this sorceress named Ione, and—"

"Ione!" gasped the old man.

"Do you know her?" asked Deco.

The old man nodded as he handed me the dark metal telescope I had looked at first. "Take this," he said slowly. "But be careful. Ione is a dark sorceress indeed, some say in league with Vulnyx, to whom she granted certain magical powers. Many have fallen under her spell and disappeared—or worse."

Deco and I looked at each other. Were we going to be next?

Chapter 9

We said good-bye to the old man and went back to the raft. This time we knew how to navigate the whirlpool. I held the paddle in place as a rudder while Deco gripped the sail, and even though the wind was blowing against us, we got through the swirling water.

Once we'd left the Strait of Fear behind us and were back on the open sea, we both fell exhausted onto the raft. The black moon shone in the dark sky, casting its eerie silvery glow on the water.

"I'll paddle first," I offered.

Deco didn't say anything. He looked away, like he was embarrassed or something. "So . . . uh . . . thanks for saving me from the sea monster—I mean whirlpool," he said before I could correct him.

"Thanks for saving me from the claw-clops," I answered. "Guess that makes us even."

"Guess so," said Deco.

After that, we were too tired to talk. I vaguely remember the wind picking up sometime later, blowing us across the sea. The next thing I knew, something was tickling my nose. I opened my eyes and saw the waves gently licking the white sand. We had drifted back to Waterfall Island.

The bright blue butterfly fluttered and landed on my hand. Seconds later, Ione appeared, butterflies flitting around her like a moving cloud of light.

"Ah, the star hunters have returned," she said in her musical voice, which, now that I knew her, no longer sounded so musical to me.

"That's right," replied Deco.

"And where is my star?" she asked as if she was sure we couldn't possibly have brought her one.

"Right in here," I said with a big smile as I held up the telescope. Ione stared from the telescope to me and then laughed. I could see she didn't believe me.

"Honest," I continued, moving toward her. "I brought you a star. See for yourself."

I stood right next to her and looked into the telescope. I made sure it was pointed at the brightest star in the sky. Then I held it still and told her to look inside. With another little laugh, she bent and peeked through the eyepiece. Her smile disappeared in an instant. I knew I had beaten her fair and square and she had no choice but to give me what I wanted.

"Now give me the bottle," I told her.

"Yeah," agreed Deco. "A deal's a deal."

I held my breath, waiting to see what Ione would do. She stared at me for a long moment without speaking. I felt like her eyes were looking right through me. Slowly, she handed me the blue bottle.

"Yes, you did complete that little quest," she said in a soft voice. "But unfortunately, that blue bottle won't save your father all by itself."

"How do you know about my father?" I gulped.

"A sorceress knows many things," she answered. "If you really want to save your father, all three bottles are absolutely necessary."

Her eyes flashed, sending silver-gold sparkles into the night.

"My father is here, alive?" I gasped.

"Yes," she replied in her singsong voice.

"Tell me where he is."

"Why should I do that?"

"I'll do anything—anything you want—if you'll tell me where my father is."

"Is that a promise?"

I nodded, barely able to breathe.

"Ione lies!" cried Deco. "Don't let her put a spell on you."

"I don't care!" I screamed. "She knows where my father is and that's all that matters."

Ione clapped her hands together in excitement, the butterflies shimmering along the length of her robe. "Well, then, it's really very simple," she answered, her eyes gleaming in anticipation. "Just give me the blue bottle—plus its two companions. When I have all three bottles in my possession, I will tell you what you are so anxious to learn." She gave me a knowing little smile.

I hesitated, wondering what to do. I remembered the flash of light I'd seen when Great-aunt Athena opened the trunk. There could have been other bottles in there. Plus, there were three bottles in the bedtime story. "I'll go get the other bottles," I answered.

Ione eyed me darkly.

"But I'll only do it if you tell me now where my father is."

Ione hesitated as if weighing my words very carefully.

"She'll never do it," murmured Deco beside me.

"All right," replied Ione, giving me an icy smile. "I tell you where your father is, and you go to your world and get the bottles."

"That's right," I said.

"Just to make sure you return to me, I'll keep your little friend as my guest," Ione added, almost as an afterthought.

"You mean prisoner," cried Deco. "No way!"

I noticed then that the crawlers were slowly moving toward us from the edge of the jungle, the green vines like snakes writhing across the white sand. I pretended not to see them, moving the blue bottle behind my back. Slowly, I took out the stopper.

The wind began to blow and the waves crashed against the shore. Not far to my right, almost exactly where I'd come through from Tiger Lily, I saw an opening in the air. And through that door I could see the raft and the pink glint of the setting sun on the dark, still water of the cove. I could just make out the opening from where I stood, but I was pretty sure that Ione couldn't.

"Do we have a deal?" asked Ione as the butterflies flapped their brightly colored wings in the sudden breeze.

"Okay, deal!" I shouted over the crashing of the waves and the roaring of the wind. "I'll get the bottles and bring them back."

"What do you think you're doing?" yelled Deco. "Are you crazy?"

He ran toward me, the crawlers slithering just yards behind him. I tripped him and he fell to the ground. With all my strength, I pinned his arm behind his back, praying the crawlers wouldn't catch him.

"Just do what I say," I whispered to him. Then I called out to Ione, "Okay, now tell me where my father is!"

The crawlers came slithering closer. They were just

feet away. If she didn't tell me soon, Deco would be her prisoner or worse.

"He's being held on Shadow Rock, off the coast of the Isle of Winds." Ione's voice drifted toward me on the wind.

I didn't waste another second. Just as the crawlers were about to entwine themselves around Deco, I shoved him through the opening in the air. The last thing I heard as we both fell through into my world was Ione shouting, "Remember to open the blue one, or . . . !"

But before I could ask her what she meant, the door between my world and the Islands of the Black Moon had already begun to disappear. In seconds it faded away altogether.

Chapter 10

"What's happening?" shouted Deco.

"Just hold on," I yelled back, clutching even more tightly to Deco's arm as we spun wildly around and around. "Grab on to me."

Deco stuck out his hand and tried to grasp some part of me, but he kept missing. Finally, he managed to grab my ankle and held it so tightly it hurt. I tried to tell him to loosen his grip, but the words got stuck in my throat as we fell into the darkness.

Splash! The cold water felt good as I kicked my way toward the surface. I came up gasping for air. There was the raft floating in the cove, and behind it, perched on the hilltop, was Tiger Lily.

"Where are we?" asked Deco, treading water beside me.

"In my world," I answered with a grin. "Follow me."

"Did Ione come after us?" asked Deco.

I shrugged. "I don't think so. Do you see her?"

We looked around as we swam to shore, but there was no sign of Ione.

"Do you know where we are exactly?" Deco repeated.

"Yep," I answered. "We're home!"

As we made our way up the hillside, I was thinking of all the things I would tell Great-aunt Athena about my adventures so far. I barely heard Deco's exclamations of surprise about the house and the grounds.

"Great-aunt Athena!" I shouted as we burst through the kitchen door.

There was no answer, just the hum of the refrigerator and, somewhere outside, the hoot of an owl.

"What are these?" asked Deco, picking up a chocolate chip cookie from a plate on the table.

"Cookies," I said without thinking.

"What do you do with them?"

"You eat them, of course," I answered. "Haven't you ever—Oh, never mind."

"There's something under the plate," said Deco, his mouth full of cookie. "Here." He handed me a note written in Great-aunt Athena's spidery scrawl.

Dear Lila,

I thought you might need a bedtime snack. I'll see you in the morning. By the way, if you need anything else, feel free to take it. As the last of the da Gamas, all will be yours one day. . . .

GAA

I looked up to see Deco standing in front of the refrigerator, chugging milk from the carton.

"Wow!" he exclaimed. "This is much easier than milking a cow."

I nodded, my eyes returning to the note. It was like Great-aunt Athena knew what had happened. And what did she mean, I was free to take whatever I needed? I stared out the darkened kitchen window toward the cove, but I couldn't see anything. I realized that the sun had just set, which meant that I had returned to Tiger Lily at the same time I left. No time had passed here in my world. I almost would have thought I imagined the whole thing, that I'd fallen asleep and dreamt the island and Ione and the rest of it, except that Deco was standing right in front of me.

"Come on," I ordered. He was experimenting with the toaster, turning it on and off, warming his hands over the electric coils.

"I've never seen a hand warmer that didn't use fire for heat," he said, looking around the kitchen in wonder. "You have so many things." He shook his head in shock. "A whole room just for eating and storing your food."

"Great-aunt Athena!" I called as we made our way up the stairs.

Still there was no answer.

"Great-aunt Athena!" I called again, more loudly, as we turned the corner on the landing and headed toward her bedroom. I knocked once and then again, harder. Still there was no answer.

Slowly, I turned the knob and pushed open the heavy wooden door. A buzzing that sounded like a lawn mower filled my ears. When I turned around, I saw why. Great-aunt Athena was lying on her back, propped up against a mountain of pillows, and she was snoring so loudly, her whole body was moving up and down with every breath.

"Great-aunt Athena," I whispered, tapping her shoulder.

But the only answer I got was another snore.

"Great-aunt Athena," I began again, more loudly. "I'm back. There's a whole bunch of stuff I need to tell you. And so many things I need to ask you . . ."

But Great-aunt Athena just kept right on snoring, and no matter how much poking and prodding I did, she remained fast asleep. She wasn't kidding about that sleeping potion—she was out like a light. I pulled the covers up to her chin and began to tiptoe out of the room. It looked as if it was up to me to figure things out. I was about to tell Deco we were on our own when I realized suddenly that he wasn't in the room.

"Deco!" I called, running out into the hall.

Only silence answered me.

"Deco, we have to—" I began, then stopped as he suddenly appeared from the direction of my room. "What were you doing?" I asked, trying not to sound exasperated.

"Nothing," he answered, sticking his hand in his pocket and not looking at me. Obviously he'd been up to something, but I didn't have time to worry about it.

"We have to get the bottles, remember?" I said. "And we have to hurry."

Deco nodded, following me down the stairs into the library. I flipped on the light, the glare making the room look even more dusty and forgotten. In three steps I was at the trunk, remembering as I stopped in front of it that I'd have to go back to Great-aunt Athena's room to find the key.

"The bottles are in there?" asked Deco beside me.

"Uh-huh," I answered. "I have to get the key."

"No, you don't," said Deco. And before I could say another word, he'd bent down and picked the lock.

"Where'd you learn to do that?" I exclaimed.

"Here and there," he answered with a grin.

I pulled up the heavy brass-cornered lid and saw the same flash of colors I'd seen before. Only this time, I saw where it was coming from. In the bottom of the trunk lay two more bottles, one yellow and one red, and they were both glowing with a strange, burning magical light. Beside them was a rolled-up piece of parchment I knew had to be the map. I brought all the stuff over to the desk.

Slowly and carefully, I unrolled the map, making sure not to rip the fragile, yellowed paper.

"See, here is Waterfall Island," I said, pointing. "Over here is Tower Island and the Strait of Fear. Now, where is Shadow Rock?"

Deco frowned, looking over my shoulder.

"It's your world, don't you know where it is?" I remarked in surprise as my eyes scanned the faded ink. "Or the Isle of Winds—Ione said it was near there."

"I told you I never been there," said Deco just as I spotted Shadow Rock on the map.

"There it is!" I exclaimed, pointing.

"Oh," said Deco, sounding surprised.

"See the words right here in the water, next to that small shape that's across from the Isle of Winds, it says . . ." I trailed off as I noticed Deco's look of total incomprehension. "You can't read, can you?"

Deco shrugged. "Nobody can, except maybe the sultan and his advisors, I guess." He reached for the yellow bottle and held it up to catch the light.

I gasped as the yellow sparkles took the shape of a tiny winged horse and hovered over the island with the three arches on it. I noticed that the Island of the Three Arches was right next to the island with the bunch of trees on it. Both islands were southwest of Tower Island. When I blinked, the yellow sparkle horse disappeared.

"Did you see that?" I gasped.

"See what?" asked Deco, still twiddling the bottle between his thumb and forefinger.

"The horse!" I exclaimed. "Over the Island of the Three Arches."

"Nope," answered Deco. "But I heard that's a very dangerous place. There's some dark, terrible forest near there, and anyone who goes in gets so lost he never comes out."

"Well, it's a sign, so I guess that means we have to—" I began as I picked up the red bottle and put it in my pocket next to the blue bottle.

But I never got to finish my sentence, because Deco chose that moment to pull the stopper out of the little yellow bottle and sniff it.

"No!" I cried.

But it was too late. The room had already begun to spin around and around, and a door had opened in the air just like the one that had appeared at the cove. Deco and I had just enough time to grasp hands before we were pulled into the hole, into whatever lay in the world beyond the door.

Chapter 11

"There they are!"

"I see them too!"

"Get them!"

I opened my eyes, blinking in the dim light. Deco and I were both sprawled on the damp, leafy floor of an immense forest. Tall trees towered over us, their branches arching together like a ceiling.

"Where are we?" I asked, staring around the gloomy forest.

"I don't know," Deco whispered, "but I think *they're* up there." He nodded toward the tops of the trees.

We stood slowly, trying to make as little noise as possible. I picked up the yellow bottle, which was lying on the ground beside Deco, and put it in my pocket next to the other two.

"This way," Deco mouthed, leading me over to a gray boulder. We crouched behind it, staring into the green darkness.

We couldn't see much of anything, but the rustling of leaves and branches all around us was unmistakable.

"Manticores?" I asked.

Deco frowned, shaking his head.

I couldn't help wondering if whoever or whatever was out there was even worse than those terrible tiger soldiers.

"Whoever they are, there's an awful lot of them," Deco said after a few more tense moments of listening to all the rustling noises. "Let's go this way."

We crept from behind the boulder and headed to the left, toward the safety of the deeper part of the forest.

"There they are!" called a voice.

"I see them again!" shouted another.

"There! There! Get them!" cackled a chorus of nasty voices, sounding even closer than before.

"We'd better run for it!" I screamed, taking off in the opposite direction.

"I told you this forest was haunted!" Deco followed close behind as we twisted and turned, stumbling over giant tree roots.

"They're moving toward the bridge!" croaked a

harsh voice that made goose bumps rise on my arms. "The intruders must be stopped!"

Deco and I put on a burst of speed. Branches scratched my face, and my breath came in ragged gasps as we struggled to keep going. Just when I thought we might be getting away, something whizzed through the air over our heads.

"Up there!" I gasped in horror, pointing. "They must be in the trees!"

"They're shooting arrows at us," Deco said as I felt a hard, sharp object graze my back.

"Run!" I cried, blindly pushing my way through the trees, now trying to find a way out of the forest and the rain of arrows.

"Ouch!" Deco yelped, dodging to the left and heading down the hillside.

I followed him, stumbling down the slope as more arrows whistled over our heads. Deco reached the bottom of the hill ahead of me. I was racing to catch him when I tripped over a branch and fell. Instead of hitting the leafy ground, I felt myself free-falling—and the next thing I knew, I hit bottom. I found myself in a deep hole with a soft, leafy bottom. I had opened my mouth to call for Deco when I saw how far above me the dim green light of the forest was. There was no way he'd hear me.

I patted my pockets, checking to make sure the three bottles were still there. Then I began the long climb back up. Making my way from stone to stone, I inched upward. As I neared the top, I heard the murmur of voices. I couldn't make out any words at first, but just as I was about to pull myself up, the voices became clear and I stopped, listening.

"Tell the others that the winged horses are safe once more. The intruders have left the forest and all shall be well, shall be well."

"Winged horses," I whispered. That was the sign I'd seen, and Great-aunt Athena had said I was supposed to follow the signs.

I inched my way to the surface to see who was speaking and how many of them there were.

"She is not the one," one of them said. The sound echoed in the empty forest.

"How can we be sure?" rasped an old, quivering voice.

"Because she ran," came the reply. "The one who will return the bottles must be brave and strong, master of her fear. Otherwise, how will she face Vulnyx?"

"Perhaps you are right," sighed the old voice. "Perhaps she is not the one."

"I think the intruders have come from Ione!" squeaked an angry voice.

My mind raced with all I was hearing. I was sure they were talking about me! I pushed myself to the surface and scrambled out of the pit, ready to address whoever was up there and reveal my identity.

But when I looked around, I was alone.

"Come out, wherever you are, and tell me where I can find the winged horses," I called into the woods, trying hard to keep the quiver out of my voice.

My words echoed in the stillness. The only answer was silence.

"Come on!" I began again. "I'm not afraid of you. I *am* the one. Now tell me where the winged horses are, or . . ." I paused, trying to think of something I could use as a threat. "Or . . ."

Then I did the only thing I could think of—I took the bottles out of my pocket and held them above my head. They caught a shaft of sunlight and sparkled in the gloomy forest like a rainbow.

"See!" I shouted. "I have the bottles. I *am* the one."

I whirled around, looking for the source of the voices. No one appeared. There was no one there— just the trees, tall and silent all around me.

"Lila, what are you doing?"

I spun and found myself face to face with Deco.

"I was looking for you," he said, holding up a skinny branch barely bigger than a twig. "This is one of the arrows they were shooting at us. What kind of fierce warriors would shoot sticks instead of real arrows?"

"I don't know," I answered, "but whoever they are, they know where the winged horses are, and I have to find them."

"But, Lila—"

"Tell me where we can find the winged horses!" I demanded in as loud and confident a voice as I could muster. "I haven't been sent by Ione—honest. I don't even know exactly how I got here, but I know I have to follow the signs. I saw a winged horse so I know I have to find one."

"Lila, whoever they are, the cowards are gone," scoffed Deco. "So—"

"I am the one!" I shouted at the top of my lungs. "I demand that you tell me where the winged horses are."

Suddenly, a breeze began to blow, the branches swayed, and leaves rustled all around as golden shafts of sunlight streaked through the woods. Deco and I blinked in the rush of light.

"Look!" exclaimed Deco, pointing in surprise up the mountain, where the trees had parted, revealing a golden path of light.

I'd had a feeling it was the trees that had been talking all along. Now they were answering me.

"Thank you!" I called.

"Let's go!" said Deco, taking a few steps along the path of light.

I followed slowly, a strange sadness in my heart that I didn't understand. Then I turned and bowed. "Good-bye!" I whispered.

No one spoke in answer, but one tiny yellow leaf drifted down and landed in my hand. I put it in my pocket and ran to catch up with Deco. We followed the sunlit path through the dark forest. When we came out the other side, we could see in the distance the ruins of three arches made of crumbling white stones.

"Where are the winged horses?" asked Deco.

"I don't know," I answered. "But I'm sure we're supposed to keep following the path."

Slowly, we made our way toward the arches. It took us a while, but when we got close enough, we saw that they were on a small island, separated from us by a shallow pool of the bluest water. Sticking up out of the water, shrouded in mist, were a bunch of rocks that formed a path to the island. Deco went first, hopping lightly from rock to rock. We could barely see because of the mist all around us. A whinnying from above drew our attention up—a flying horse was diving straight for us!

"The horses! They're flying right at us!" shouted Deco. "Make a run for it!"

We both dashed across the final few rocks and threw ourselves to the ground just in time. We felt the cool currents of air generated by the flapping of the horses' giant wings. A few seconds later, we heard the horses land somewhere close by. The mist lifted then, and we saw the herd for the first time. We stood slowly, awed by the beautiful, majestic creatures before us. They were pure white with amber eyes, and they had the most incredible snowy wings.

I remembered the sign. "Maybe one of those flying

horses will take us to Shadow Rock," I said, thinking aloud.

"That's the one we want," Deco said, pointing to the largest one, which stood beneath the arches. "It'll be the fastest." And he charged headlong toward the huge white animal.

"Deco, don't!" I shouted.

But it was too late. As Deco reached the giant winged creature, it reared high in the air and knocked him to the ground with its powerful golden hooves. Deco jumped up and began to chase the white horse, while the other winged beasts snorted and stamped their feet.

"Stop, Deco!" I cried again.

But he didn't listen. Instead, he climbed onto the tallest boulder in the clearing, and as the great white creature galloped toward him, he jumped onto its back. He flung his arms around its neck, his hands gripping the flowing white mane. The horse reared high in the air, its immense wings flapping so hard that I felt the breeze where I stood. Before I could move, the horse broke into a gallop, its long legs moving so fast they were like a white blur in the sunlight. The faster the horse ran, the tighter Deco's knees dug into its massive sides. He looked terrified. Suddenly, the great white creature stopped and lowered its head toward the rocky ground.

Deco went flying through the air and crashed into the crumbling stone steps leading up to the central arch. Above him rose the only tree that grew in the desolate spot, its branches gnarled and twisted, its leaves withered with age.

"Deco!" I cried, running toward him. "Deco, get up!"

But Deco didn't move. He lay still, his eyes closed, his body sprawled in a heap on the rocks.

"Deco, wake up!" I murmured, shaking him gently. But he lay still, barely breathing.

"Deco, you can't die!" I cried. "It's all my fault."

The tears came, running hot and salty down my cheeks. "Deco, I'm so sorry," I murmured. "It's all my fault. If you'd never met me, you'd be . . ." I couldn't bear to finish the thought.

When I looked up, I saw that the horses had drifted toward the center of the arches where there was a bit of grass. At a signal from the great white horse, they tucked their wings in at their sides, lowered their heads, and began to graze. I had to do something to save Deco, but what? I jumped to my feet, pacing in front of the rocks. I stuck my hand in my pocket and my fingers touched something smooth and papery light. I pulled it out. It was the yellow leaf from the forest. I twirled the leaf in my hand as I rocked back and forth over Deco's still body.

"I never should have come," I said, my words echoing in the quiet afternoon. "I've made a mess of everything. I just want to go home." And not to Tiger Lily, I thought sadly, back home to Mom. Great-aunt

Athena was right. I wasn't ready. I should never have opened the blue bottle in the first place.

"I see by the leaf you hold that you have been sent by the old yellow tree," said a high, reedy voice. I looked up, wondering where the voice was coming from. "So I will help you with the winged horses."

"Where are you?" I asked, my eyes darting left and then right, seeing nothing but the horses grazing in the distance.

"Up here," the voice answered, and I realized in surprise that it was the twisted tree talking. "Listen closely, because my voice will not last for long. At sunset the horses quiet down, preparing for the peace of sleep. Go to them then. Stand before the great white, bow once, and stare him in the eyes. You must not blink even once, or show any fear, or the horse will attack."

I gulped as the tree continued.

"It is a fine line between fear and courage, and the horses know. Your friend was brave, but he became afraid. The great white felt his fear. The horses know that the one who rides them must have true courage to go to Shadow Rock and fulfill the destiny of the bottles."

"Shadow Rock!" I murmured in surprise. So the bottles had to be returned to the exact place where I had to go to find my father. I just hoped I was brave enough to really and truly be the one.

"As for your friend, you may revive him, but not until you have faced the great white."

"So, if I fail, he dies," I said in a whisper.

The tree didn't reply right away. Then it spoke again in an even softer voice, which I had to strain to hear. "If you succeed with the great white, three drops of juice from a red lemon will save your friend."

"A red lemon?" I blurted out. "Where am I going to get a red lemon?"

"I am a red lemon tree," the tree answered in its reedy voice.

I stood and looked carefully at the tree. One red lemon hung from a drooping branch.

"But it's the only lemon you've got," I said.

"I know," the tree responded. "One is all you need. And you may have it—if the great white allows it. To take it now, though, without her consent, would be a grave mistake."

"Thank you," I said. "How can I ever repay you?"

"Fulfill your destiny." And the tree said nothing more. I paced back and forth, waiting for the sun to set. After a while, the horses gathered in the center of the arches, clustered around the great white. Moments later, as if on cue, the sun changed from yellow to orange to a deep red as it began to sink behind the arches. I took one last look at Deco's still body. This is it, I thought as I walked toward the great white. The creature remained frozen, its golden eyes never leaving my face. I marched right up to it, bowed once, and stared into those amber eyes without blinking, trying to keep up my courage and swallow my fear. My heart was hammering away in my chest, but every time I started feeling scared, I made myself think of Deco, and that made me strong again.

A minute passed. And then another. And finally, the creature looked away and shook its great white head. I closed my eyes, waiting for the attack. But it never came. Instead, I felt something cold nuzzling my cheek. I looked up to find one of the smaller horses standing in front of me. The little horse gave a snort and turned and pranced toward Deco, looking back at me and whinnying as if telling me to come too. Amazed that I was still alive, I mutely followed the little creature.

She led me to the tree and nuzzled my hand. I reached for the red lemon and raced back to Deco. I cut a small hole in the top of the lemon with Deco's boomerang, then squeezed the fruit over his mouth. One drop. Then another. And then a third, just as the tree had instructed.

Nothing happened at first, and then Deco's eyes slowly opened. He sat up, rubbing his head.

"What happened?" he asked.

"It's a long story," I answered with a smile. "Let's just say you have a lot to thank this little red lemon for—like your life."

"Really?" said Deco as he stretched out a hand for the lemon.

"Uh-huh," I answered. "I'll tell you all about it on the way to Shadow Rock." Now I knew just how we were going to get there.

The little horse, as if it understood me, flapped its white wings and lay down at our feet.

Chapter 12

Flying on the little winged horse was fun at first. With the cool night air on our faces, we soared through the clouds, bathed in the black moon's silvery light. But after a while, my arms began to cramp from holding so tightly to the creature's soft, silky neck, and my legs grew stiff from gripping its sides. I could feel Deco tiring too, his arms loosening their hold around my waist.

I must have closed my eyes for a minute, because the next thing I knew the horse was descending. Could we be at Shadow Rock already? I wondered.

We burst through the clouds and found ourselves above a city, its buildings tiny dots far below us.

"That's not Shadow Rock, is it?" I shouted.

"No," Deco shouted back, grabbing me more tightly around the waist. "We definitely don't want to land there! That would be a big mistake."

As we descended, I could see the outlines of houses and blurry dark lines I thought must be streets. "Is this Bell Isle?" I yelled in Deco's ear.

"Yes!" he shouted as a golden dome came into view below us. "We've got to make it stop!"

"What's that?" I asked, pointing.

"The sultan's palace," Deco answered. "If we go there, we're dead."

Maybe the horse understood what Deco had said. Or maybe it already had something else in mind, because it veered away from the palace and flew over the city toward a thin strip of beach in the distance. The horse suddenly nose-dived, heading for a stand of trees. Deco and I both hung on for our lives.

"We're going to crash!" I shrieked as the trees rushed up toward us.

But then, when we were so close I could make out the shapes of individual leaves, the horse shifted to the left. It slowed down and gently drifted through an opening that suddenly appeared in the trees, and landed soundlessly on the ground.

Deco and I sat there for a moment, too shocked to move.

"I can't believe—" I began just as Deco said, "That was sure—"

Then we both laughed and the horse tossed its

head and whinnied, its white mane gleaming in the moonlit clearing. We stood and stretched, looking around.

"Where are we?" I asked.

"Beats me," answered Deco.

The horse walked forward, deeper into the trees. Deco and I shrugged and followed. The horse turned this way and that like it knew exactly where it was going. A few moments later, we found ourselves in front of a small stone hut. Deco knocked on the door. There was no answer, although we saw smoke coming from the chimney.

"Whatever's cooking sure smells good," said Deco, wrinkling his nose in appreciation. "Let's go inside and have some. I'm starved."

"We can't just go into someone else's house and take their food," I retorted hotly.

"Quit being so prissy," said Deco, slowly opening the door.

I don't know what I expected. For a scientific person, I was certainly having some pretty crazy ideas. I kept thinking of the story of Hansel and Gretel and the witch in the gingerbread house in the woods. The skin on the back of my neck prickled as I stared from the hut to the tall trees looming up darkly all around me.

"Wait!" I cried.

But it was too late. Deco had already disappeared through the crude wooden door. It looked like I had no choice but to follow him.

"Look!" he said, his eyes shining. "A fish!"

Roasting on a spit over the fire was indeed a large fish. My stomach grumbled at the smell of it. I hate fish as a rule, but I was so hungry anything probably would have looked good to me. Deco reached out for a piece and stuffed it in his mouth.

"Don't, Deco!" I said.

Seconds later, he spit it out.

"Wow! That's hot!" he exclaimed. "It burned my mouth."

I was about to say "I told you so" when the door suddenly slammed behind us. We both jumped. Standing on the threshold of the room was a tall, stooped figure dressed in a dark cloak. A hood covered its face so that in the flickering firelight all we could see were the eyes. They were such a pale shade of blue, they looked almost white. My mouth opened in a wide O of horror as I felt Deco stiffen beside me.

"Welcome," said the old man in a rasping voice, staring at us intently with those weird pale eyes. "I see that you are hungry, so please, eat."

"Thank you, but we were just leaving," I replied in as calm a voice as I could muster.

The tall old man shrugged off his cloak like I hadn't spoken, shaking out his long, straight silver hair. He turned to me, and when I looked into his eyes, I saw they weren't as scary as I'd thought at first. They were actually sad, as if he'd seen so many terrible things in his lifetime there was nothing left to surprise him. Deco was already eating happily, so with a sigh I sat down too.

"Who are you?" I asked.

"Once I was called the Keeper," replied the old man in a soft voice. "But as what I kept is no longer in my keeping, the name no longer rightfully belongs to me."

"The Keeper?" I repeated, my heart beating faster in my chest as I remembered what Ione had said about the man in the boat who had given the bottles to my ancestor Vasco da Gama. "Keeper of what?" I held my breath, wondering if he could possibly be the man in the bedtime story.

The old man took another bite of fish, his eyes on the fire. "I was the Keeper of three special bottles, which held within them the wishes, hopes, and dreams of all the islands."

"Was one blue, one red, and one yellow?" I asked in a whisper.

The old man nodded without looking at me. "Yes, that's right."

"So what exactly happened to these bottles?" I went on.

"Fifty years ago, when I was a much younger man, the sultan of the islands had an evil advisor named Vulnyx, who was conspiring to steal the sultan's power. With the help of a sorceress named Ione, he cast a spell on the sultan and on the sultan's army, turning them from men into fearsome creatures who would follow his every evil order without question. Then Vulnyx had Ione give him the wings of a vulture, and he flew to Shadow Rock to steal the bottles."

The Keeper paused, staring into the fire. Deco and I looked at each other, our eyes wide.

"So then what happened?" I asked.

"A See-It-All bird informed me of what was happening. Just before Vulnyx got there, I removed the bottles from their special positions in Shadow Rock. Then I broke the sacred code of sorcery and created a door between the worlds and sent the bottles to safety. In doing so, however, I lost my powers forever."

"So that's why Ione couldn't follow us through the door to Lila's world!" Deco exclaimed. "If she did she would lose her power!"

The Keeper turned, startled, his pale eyes moving from Deco to me.

"You know Ione?" he said, his eyes narrowing. "Have you come as her—"

"No, she's after us, actually," I said, pulling the bottles out of my pocket. "Because we have them—the bottles you're talking about. Here, look."

I placed the three bottles on the table before the Keeper, who stared at them without saying a word. After a minute, he put out one wrinkled hand to touch them.

"Five hundred years ago by your time," he began, nodding at me, "I gave these bottles to a sea captain, who came through the door in the air I had created. I instructed him to look for signs, which would show when it was time to bring them back."

"I'm pretty sure that sea captain you gave the bottles to was my ancestor Vasco da Gama," I said slowly. "He lived five hundred years ago. I guess I'm the one, since I saw the signs, which is how I wound up here in the first place—"

"Wait a minute," interrupted Deco, staring at the Keeper. "That means you're really, really old. I mean, if you were around five hundred years ago and everything."

"Not that old," replied the old man with a chuckle. "You see, time in your friend's world is ten times faster than time in our world. I gave the bottles to the captain exactly fifty years ago by our time, which makes me going on ninety now. That's old enough, but not so ancient. I had begun to doubt I would live to see the bottles returned at all."

"So now what are we supposed to do with the bottles, exactly?" I asked. "I mean, once we bring them back to Shadow Rock?"

"First you must contend with Vulnyx, who I'm told guards Shadow Rock, waiting for the bottles to be returned," answered the Keeper. "According to his evil plan, he expects them to be brought back by Ione so that he can place them in an ancient stone circle carved into the stone in the heart of a maze. That way, he will keep the world of the islands in his dark power. But if you are able to get past him and place the bottles yourself, then Vulnyx will lose his power."

"I don't understand how three bottles could make such a big difference."

The Keeper let out a long sigh. "When the Islands of the Black Moon first came into being, at the very beginning of time when darkness and chaos reigned, there lived three wise old sorcerers. Some say they conjured the islands out of the depths of the sea by their very powers. Regardless, each of these three sorcerers put all of his wishes, hopes, and dreams, all of the goodness and light in his heart, into each of the three bottles. For they wanted for the people who would one day come to live on the islands what did not exist anywhere at that time—happiness. Then they hid the bottles in the place now known as Shadow Rock. And then they disappeared.

"And as those old sorcerers had willed, happiness reigned on the Islands of the Black Moon for many, many years, until the day I sent the bottles away. So you see, the bottles must be returned in order for joy and light to return too, but they must be placed in their age-old positions by one pure of heart. If Vulnyx puts the bottles back, darkness will reign as it once did in the long-ago past and all of the hopes, wishes, and dreams of the three sorcerers will be lost forever."

"So that's why Ione wanted the bottles?" I asked.

The Keeper nodded. "Now you can see why you must not let her have them—no matter what."

I gulped, thinking of how close I'd come to handing over the bottles to that evil creature.

"How do we get through the maze?" asked Deco.

The old man frowned. "You must bring a piece of the sun with you to light your way. Without light you will never be able to negotiate the darkness and find your way to the center of the maze."

I thought about what the old man had said.

"You must be very careful," he warned after a few minutes. "Shadow Rock is a wild, stormy place, and it's easy to be dashed to pieces against the rocks. That is why the bottles were kept there, because the land itself protected them. When you see the circle at the maze's center, you will notice that there is a triangle within its heart, with a hole at each point. In each hole you must place the bottle that belongs there."

"Which one goes where?" I asked.

He put his finger to his lips. "First the blue one, then . . ." He cocked his head, listening. I heard nothing but the silence of the forest all around us, but the old man was frowning and I saw a worried look in his eyes.

"You must go now," he said quickly, jumping to his feet. "Climb out the window, mount the horse, and fly into the night." He put his hand on my shoulder and stared into my eyes with his strange pale ones. "Only you can do what must be done."

I nodded and with a whispered thanks crawled out the window, with Deco behind me. The horse was grazing where we'd left it by the side of the hut. Quickly we hopped on its back, and it took instantly to the air. Not a moment too soon, for I caught sight of a butterfly, then another. And into the clearing flew Ione, borne along by the butterflies.

"Give me the bottles!" she commanded, staring up at us, her firecracker eyes shooting colored sparkles into the night.

"Never!" I cried as the horse circled higher over her head.

"You'll be sorry," she called, her black hair billowing around her like the dark of night itself. "You promised."

"I promised I'd bring the bottles back, not that I'd give them to you," I yelled at the same moment that the old man appeared in the doorway of the hut.

He called to Ione, his hands waving in the air. I wondered what he was doing; then I spotted the golden bow in her hands.

"Oh, no!" I shouted, kicking my heels into the horse's sides.

"Hurry!" echoed Deco, kicking the horse too.

The horse soared upward, but not fast enough. One golden arrow pierced its leg, its blood crimson in the light of the black moon.

Chapter 13

After we'd flown some distance away, Deco and I urged the horse to land. Its leg was still bleeding, and we were both worried. But it kept going, flying through the dark night even faster than before.

"Look!" called Deco, pointing down at a range of mountain peaks that had just appeared through the clouds. "I bet we're close."

I nodded. As I stared down, I noticed how tall and jagged the peaks looked. I also saw that the clouds that had been silvery white before were now gray. The closer we got to the mountains, the darker the clouds became.

"We should bear to the left when we hit the peaks," called Deco.

"No, go right," I called back.

"No, left!" shouted Deco.

Before I could reply, the winged horse swerved sharply to the left and flapped its massive wings, soaring up. The dark clouds swallowed us, obscuring our vision. The next thing we knew, there was a sickening thud as something slammed into the horse. We spun away out of control, like a car when it's been sideswiped.

"Aahhh!" I screamed as the horse began to free-fall.

I tightened my grip on the creature's neck just as Deco grabbed me.

"What was that?" I cried, peering into the shadowy clouds.

"We must have hit something," said Deco in a panicky voice.

The horse struggled to stop falling. Finally, it managed to regain its balance, but its wings beat more slowly and its breath came in ragged gasps. As we soared upward, the clouds thinned for a moment and I caught a glimpse of something with big, black wings. On one of the mountain peaks was something huge and black that looked like a vulture. It was too far away to see clearly, but I didn't have to get any closer to know it must be Vulnyx.

"We didn't hit something!" I shouted. "Something hit us!"

I pointed to the peak, where the evil creature was

spreading its wings and lifting itself into the air. It didn't fly at us this time. Instead, it descended lower and lower until it disappeared into the swirling black clouds below us.

"Where did it go?" asked Deco as he stared down, desperately trying to spot the vulture man.

"I don't know," I screamed, peering into the black bank of fog and clouds, dread lodged in the pit of my stomach like a boulder.

At that moment, there was a rush of air, and there it was above us, wings extended, its one glassy blue eye glaring right at us, rimmed with angry red.

I clutched the winged horse desperately around the neck and tucked my legs tightly, pressing my knees into its sides. We began to descend so rapidly we were flying at a forty-five-degree angle.

"Hold on!" I screamed.

Vulnyx descended even more quickly than we did, his talons pointed right at us. With an extra flap of his wings, he swooped down and grabbed Deco in his razor-sharp yellow claws.

"Deco!" I watched in terror as Vulnyx carried him farther and farther into the sky. I was sure Deco was going to be dashed against the rocks, but he hung on, his face a white blur in the darkness.

"Follow me," commanded Vulnyx as he again dove toward the ground.

"Deco, hang on!" I cried. "I'm coming!"

I was frantic, trying to figure out what I could do

to save him, as my knees dug into the white horse's side and we flew downward. Suddenly, Vulnyx righted himself from his nosedive. Spreading his wings wide, he began to glide down through the dark bank of clouds. I urged the white horse to follow, praying that Deco was all right.

Vulnyx touched down on a small patch of dead brown grass, bordered on one side by a forest of gray leafless trees, and on the other by a steep rock face. I had to crane my neck to see the top of Shadow Rock. Just looking at it made me shiver. As soon as the white horse landed, I jumped off and ran over to where Deco lay in the shadows, sprawled on the ground before Vulnyx.

Seeing Vulnyx up close scared me so much, it took every ounce of courage I had to stand my ground. Vulnyx was worse than I had ever imagined, a horrible hunchbacked figure in a long, moth-eaten black cape. His face was white as paste, and he was staring at me with his one glassy blue eye. As he moved closer, I shuddered. What I'd thought was a cloak was actually a pair of ragged black wings, and instead of hands and feet he had long, pointy yellow talons.

"Please allow me to introduce myself," said the vulture-man in a voice as smooth as silk, a total contrast with his monstrous appearance. "I am Vulnyx. And this, as you must have guessed, is Shadow Rock."

"You'd better let my friend go right this minute or . . ." My voice trailed off as I tried to think of what I could possibly do to this horrible creature.

"Or you'll what?" prompted Vulnyx, and then he laughed a chilling laugh. "He is free to go whenever he chooses. You, however, must do something for me—if you ever want to see your father again."

Deco jumped up and ran toward me, and we both backed as far away from Vulnyx as possible.

"My father?" I gasped. "Where is my father?"

"I made things simple for you, Lila da Gama," replied Vulnyx, moving closer so that I could smell his nasty, dead-smelling breath. "Your father is in the center of the maze, right where the bottles need to go, right where the terrors lurk."

"Terrors?" I asked.

Vulnyx nodded, his blue eye pinning me in its cold, glassy gaze. "That's right, terrors. When you see them, you will know fear as you've never known it before."

"Why are you telling us all this?" Deco asked, frowning.

"Yeah," I said. "We know you want the bottles for yourself. Why don't you just take them?"

"Why?" echoed Vulnyx. "Because only one who is pure of heart may enter the center of the maze, bearing the bottles. And a pure heart, alas, is something I do not possess. That is where you come in, Lila."

"How do you know I'll do it?" I countered.

"Because you love your father and you would do anything to save him."

He was right, of course.

"It's really very simple," continued Vulnyx. "You

bring the bottles to the center of the maze and I'll let your father go—if you manage to survive, naturally."

A soft moan made Deco and me both turn. The white horse was half standing and half lying in the grass. Its amber eyes were glazed with pain, and blood was running down its injured leg.

"We have to clean the wound," I said, running over to it.

I tore a strip of cloth from the bottom of my T-shirt and gently cleaned the blood from the horse's leg. With the blood gone, the wound didn't look so bad. I was about to say so when the horse suddenly collapsed at my feet. It stared at me and slowly closed its eyes.

"Deco, quick, we've got to do something!" I cried.

"There is nothing you can do," came Vulnyx's creepy voice. "It was a poison arrow. Now the maze awaits and you must go."

Before Deco or I could move a muscle, Vulnyx came toward us, his black wings raised, his pale face like a death mask as he moved closer and closer to his prey.

Chapter 14

Vulnyx grasped each of us by the collar with one of his horrible yellow talons.

"Shall we go?" he said, pulling us away from the winged horse.

He led us through the creepy forest until we reached a massive black wooden door cut into the stone of Shadow Rock itself. It was locked with big, rusty iron bolts.

There was a rasping sound as Vulnyx drew the bolts of the ancient door and yanked it open. Beyond the door all I could see was darkness—endless, yawning blackness. I gulped and glanced at Deco, who stared back, his eyes wide in his pale face. Vulnyx turned to us then with the most evil smile I had ever seen curling up the corners of his thin, black lips.

Before we could say anything, he shoved us through the doorway. We heard the grating of metal as the bolts were drawn, leaving us with no way out. We stood frozen in total darkness as wind howled all around us. I tried to say something, but my words were snatched away by the wind. Eventually, the wind died down. I dropped to my hands and knees. The floor was cold, wet stone, but when I stretched out my hands, I felt nothing but empty space. I heard Deco moving somewhere beside me.

"Deco, get down!" I shouted. "The floor's not solid. There are huge holes."

"What?" said Deco. "Why would there be holes in the—"

But he never finished his sentence.

"Aahh!" he cried from somewhere to my left.

Reaching out carefully in the darkness, following the sound of his voice, I felt for his hand. He was hanging on to the edge of a hole. He held on while I struggled to pull him out. I wished more than ever that we had some light. If only I'd brought a flashlight. I had a whole bunch of them at home in my dresser drawer.

"If only we had some light," said Deco, echoing my thoughts. "A piece of the sun, like the Keeper said."

"I know," I replied with a sinking feeling in my stomach. Without light, going farther into the maze looked pretty much like suicide.

"It's too bad the thing I took from your house won't make light here," said Deco after a minute.

"What thing that made light?" I blurted out, trying to stay calm and keep my hopes from rising. "A flashlight?"

"I don't know," said Deco. "I tried it before when we were in the Forest of the Talking Trees, and it didn't work."

"Give it to me," I urged.

Deco handed me something small and rectangular, made of smooth plastic. It sure didn't feel like a flashlight. I wasn't sure what it was until I felt the outline of a small lightbulb. My night-light!

"This isn't any good," I said. "It's not a flashlight, it's a night-light. And you need electricity to make a night-light work."

"Electricity?" Deco repeated, confused. "What is that? Can't we make some?"

"It's the flow of electrons—particles with a negative charge," I replied without thinking. "And no, we can't just make some."

"Well, how do electrons make light? If they can, can't we?"

"They don't," I answered. "I mean, you need electrodes, which are pieces of metal that collect or release electrons in an electric circuit."

"Huh?" said Deco.

"It's hard to explain," I said, shaking my head. "See, I made a lemon battery for school last year and it

101

generated just enough voltage to light up a little light-bulb, which is really, really hard to do—I mean, it took me a bunch of times to get it to work. Anyway, the electrons traveled through the juice of the lemon, which is a great electrolyte—I mean, a substance that conducts electricity—and then one wire had a positive charge and the other one had a negative charge and bam, I made light. But we don't have a lemon or—"

"Yes, we do," burst out Deco. "I kept the lemon from the forest. Since it saved my life, I thought it was a good thing to have. So now we can make light, right?"

"Hey, wait a minute!" I exclaimed, getting excited myself. "Maybe we can."

Carefully, I unscrewed the lightbulb from the night-light.

"Here, hold this," I ordered, feeling for Deco's hand in the darkness.

"What are you going to do?" he asked.

I didn't answer. Instead I smashed the night-light's plastic casing against the stone.

"Why did you do that?" exclaimed Deco. "Now it'll never work."

"You'll see," I said, pulling off the plastic and feeling for the wires looped inside. "I hope," I added under my breath.

"What can I do?" asked Deco after a few minutes.

"Just wait." I squatted down and tried to separate the wires. It was hard work in the dark, and my fingers were sweating because I was nervous. I couldn't be sure there were even steel and copper wires in the night-light. If there weren't, we were out of luck, because those are the metals you need to create a positive and negative charge. But I pushed that thought out of my mind and kept carefully pulling the wires apart.

"What about the lemon?" asked Deco. "Do you need it yet?"

"No," I said. "But why don't you roll it on the ground once or twice? Just don't let it fall into a hole. If you roll it, that way it'll be nice and juicy. The more lemon juice we have, the better."

After carefully separating the wires, I realized there were five in all.

"Give me your boomerang," I ordered.

Holding the boomerang steady, I bared both ends of each wire, straining to see them in the darkness, even though I knew it was useless.

"Now what?" asked Deco.

"Cut the lemon in half," I said, giving him the boomerang.

"You're going to make light," said Deco, unable to hide the excitement in his voice. "A piece of the sun that burns without fire!"

"I don't know, Deco," I murmured, suddenly overcome with doubt. "I told you I'd try, but from a scientific point of view the odds are not too good. Anyway, the one time I did this I had a whole bunch more lemons, plus I had pennies for the copper part and paper clips to hold them in place and zinc—"

"Just try, Lila," urged Deco. "I believe the light will work."

"Believing in something doesn't make it real," I said.

"How do you know?" countered Deco. "You didn't believe in the sea monster, but it still almost killed us."

"That wasn't a sea monster," I said. "I told you it was a whirlpool."

"Whirlpool's just your word for sea monster," said Deco.

"Okay, Deco," I replied. "Now I need to insert one end of each wire into the lemon halves, and then I have to hook each one up to the base of the light. We'll have to try it with each wire, since one has to be copper and one has to be steel in order to create the positive and negative charges."

Deco held out the lemon halves, and I carefully hooked up the wires.

"Now the lightbulb," I said.

Deco held out the bulb, and I connected one wire and then the other to the base. Nothing happened.

"Okay, next wire," I said.

I worked my way through each combination of wires, but nothing worked. Finally, I was down to the last possibility.

"This is our last chance," I said, so frustrated I felt like I could cry. It wasn't fair. It just wasn't fair. We were so close.

"Tell me you believe you can make light," whispered Deco.

"I believe I can make light," I said. "Are you happy now?"

"Uh-huh," answered Deco.

Slowly, I stuck the wires into the lemon halves. Then I hooked one up to the bulb.

"This is it," I said. Carefully, I twisted the second wire into place—and lo and behold, the bulb lit up. The light was faint, barely enough to see more than a few feet ahead of us, but it was light.

"You did it!" cried Deco.

The two of us danced around for a minute. Then we quickly sobered, remembering our mission. And by the dim glow of the lemon light, careful to watch for holes in the stone floor, we took our first steps into the maze.

☾

The farther we ventured down that first long, dark passage, the colder and wetter it got. The darkness also seemed to get thicker, and our little light looked as tiny as a firefly. Cautiously, I led us around another big pit in the center of the floor, trying not to think about how creepy this place was.

"Hey," I said, stopping so suddenly that Deco

bumped into me. "I just thought of something. How are we going to find our way back out?"

We stood in silence for a few minutes, listening to the eerie dripping of water along the old stone walls.

"I know," said Deco, pulling out his boomerang. "I'll carve an X into a rock at the entrance to each passage we go down. That way, we'll know where we've been and we'll be able to follow the trail of X's back out."

"Good idea," I said.

We headed down the long, drafty corridor. At the end, the passage split into three.

"Which way?" I asked.

Deco shrugged. "Let's try the middle one."

The next hallway was long and twisting. The wind was stronger here, howling around our ears. I had to take tiny steps, fighting the current, doing my best to make sure the fragile wires of the lemon battery didn't disconnect. At the next fork, we went right. Deco marked another rock with his boomerang, and we went down that passage and then the next. Each time there was more than one way to go, Deco notched another X. We went down one hallway after another. I began to feel dizzy and totally confused, wondering at each new passage if we were ever going to make it to the center of the maze or if we were doomed to walk in circles forever.

"Look," said Deco, pointing as we reached the next fork. "There's an X. That means we've been here before."

With a sigh, we headed through the doorway we hadn't gone through before. And then the next and the next. Every passage looked the same. Dark and wet. It was hard to tell how much time had passed, but I could have sworn that our light was getting dimmer. I didn't want to say anything to Deco, but I had no idea how long the lemon battery would last. I mean, a lemon only has so much juice, and without the electrolyte to circulate the current, there could be no light.

We turned into the darkest, wettest, scariest passage yet. The wailing of the wind was loud here, an eerie shrieking that sounded alive. Holding tightly to the light, I moved closer to Deco. He must have sensed something too, because his footsteps slowed and he kept glancing over his shoulder like he thought we were being followed. I took a deep breath and kept going, trying to blot out the horrible feeling. At the end of the passage, we both stopped dead in our tracks.

A door rose before us, an ancient black wooden door that was bolted just like the entrance to the maze. Deco and I looked at each other, and slowly he pulled back the bolt, then gently pushed open the door. The wind stopped gusting and the howling fell silent. Before we could lose our nerve, we stepped over the threshold into whatever lay beyond the black door. With a loud clank, it slammed behind us. Worse than that, the lemon battery's wires popped apart and our light went out, just when we needed it most.

Chapter 15

I gasped, peering into the darkness. The silence echoed in my ears.

"Deco, where are you?" The words rushed out in a frightened squeak.

I reached out to touch him, but there was nothing—just empty space. Where did he go? I wondered in panic.

"Deco!" I shouted, but the word came out as a whisper. I felt like I was in one of those nightmares where you try to scream but no sound comes out. "Deco!" I tried again a bit more loudly.

"I'm right here!" he said behind me.

I whirled around and grabbed him with my free hand, the other still clutching the lemon battery.

"Deco, I thought you—" I began, relief flooding me.

"You have to fix the light," interrupted Deco just as a strange scuttling sound began. It was coming from the floor and seemed to be getting closer.

"What is that?" I whispered as a shiver went up and down my spine.

"I don't know," Deco answered.

I felt something crawling up my leg, something small and hairy, and jumped back, trying to shake the thing off. But another one was on my arm, and then another was on my leg, and more were crawling on the ground at my feet. Whatever they were, they had lots of legs and moved really fast.

"Spiders!" I screamed.

The noise grew louder and louder as more and more of them scuttled toward us.

"There are hundreds of 'em!" shouted Deco, waving his arms to shake them off.

"Aaahh!" I screamed.

"Fix the light," shouted Deco.

I shuddered, stifling another scream. Deco was right. Praying that the lemon battery had some juice left, I fumbled with the wires. But I couldn't stop the trembling in my hands as more and more spiders crawled up my legs and arms. All I wanted to do was drop everything so I could shake off the horrible creatures.

"Look out!" screamed Deco.

I whirled around. Something with glowing green eyes as big as saucers was stalking toward us. In the creepy light its eyes cast, we could see that it was larger than a bull and very hairy. It was panting loudly, its green tongue hanging out of its mouth, its teeth big and black and pointy. Deco and I both jumped backward as something swooped low over our heads. Looking up, we caught a glimpse of burning red eyes and a long, slithering serpent's tail. I stood frozen, staring at the creatures in horror.

"The light!" screamed Deco. "We need the light."

Even though my hand was shaking, I managed to attach one end of one wire. Just three more to go. I could feel hot, horrible-smelling breath on the back of my neck.

"What is it?" I cried.

"A basilisk!" screamed Deco. "Its breath is poisonous. Watch out!"

We both ducked as the thing swiped at our heads.

"Hurry, Lila!" shouted Deco, just as another basilisk dove toward us. I felt its claws skim my hair.

Using every ounce of concentration I had left, I rehooked the second, third, and fourth wires. The light still didn't work, so I switched the third wire with the first. That did it. Our little lemon battery glowed to life again. In the sudden rush of light, the creatures screeched and screamed away, disappearing into the darkness. I noticed a dim red glow coming from somewhere up ahead.

"Well done," came Vulnyx's slimy voice. "Now come and see what is really at stake for you, Lila."

"How'd he get here?" whispered Deco.

"Remember, he's a vulture," I whispered back as the two of us moved toward the sound of the voice. "He probably flew down from the top of the rocks or something."

As we rounded the corner, I saw what was making the red glow. My father was hanging upside down from a rope that was swinging slowly over a boiling pit of lava. Vulnyx was grasping the rope with one sharp yellow claw. As soon as he saw us, he lowered my father even closer to the deadly pit. Ione stood on my father's other side, her silvery-golden eyes shooting firecracker sparkles in the dim room, the butterflies fluttering around her.

"Now, be a good girl and give me the bottles," commanded Vulnyx, pinning me with his one dead blue eye. "Or your father will die a terrible death, burned beyond recognition by boiling lava. His screams of agony will echo in your ears to the end of your days."

"Don't do it, Lila." My father's deep, warm voice, the voice I had been hoping to hear for so long, flowed over me. "Don't give him the bottles!"

"Dad!" I cried. "You really are alive!"

"Enough of your dramatics, Valentine da Gama," said Vulnyx with a sneer. "For that little outburst, you will pay." With a flourish, Vulnyx lowered the rope even farther, so that my father was now swinging barely a foot above the flaming, bubbling pit.

"Stop!" I screamed. "I'll give you what you want. I don't care."

"Lila!" shouted my father. "Don't. You must place the bottles in the circle in the center of the floor. If you don't and Vulnyx does, darkness will reign through all the islands."

I stopped, hesitating, my eyes scanning the dusty gray stones. Just as my father had said, there was a circle carved in the floor, and in it were three depressions in the shape of a triangle. They looked just about the right size to hold the bottles. Even though I'd promised the Keeper I would place the bottles in the sacred circle, I couldn't let Vulnyx kill my father. I just couldn't.

"Give us the bottles, Lila," crooned Ione. I turned to her, drawn by that musical voice, noticing with surprise that she was holding the telescope I had given her. "And give me the piece of the sun you hold in your hand."

Ione came floating toward me, the butterflies shimmering in the air. Her eyes held me in their magical gaze, and without realizing what I was doing, I stepped toward her.

"Lila, no!" cried my father.

"I thought I told you to keep quiet!" Vulnyx growled as he lowered the rope so that my father swung just inches from the hissing, boiling pit.

"No!" I screamed. "Stop! I'll give them to you!"

In a panic, I turned to Deco, my eyes wild. He nodded once slowly.

Taking a deep breath, I pulled the bottles out of my pocket. I held them out toward Ione, the glass sparkling magically in the red glow. "Here they are!" I cried. "Just let my father go!"

At that moment, Deco pulled his boomerang from his belt and raised it over his head.

"Stop him!" cried Vulnyx.

But it was too late. Deco aimed and threw the boomerang just as my father swung out beyond the rim of the lava pit. The boomerang sliced through the rope and my father tumbled to the floor. I knew then just what I had to do.

"Give me the bottles!" Vulnyx shrieked.

He ran toward me, but I was too fast for him. Quickly, I bent and put the blue bottle in the first hole, the yellow in the next, and the red in the third.

Nothing happened.

"Now what?" I cried as Vulnyx swooped toward me, yellow claws raised. Behind him, I could see Deco clinging to Ione's robe. She was doing her best to shake him off, but he wasn't letting go. My father, meanwhile, was frantically untying the rope that still bound him.

I took a deep breath, trying to remember what the Keeper had said. He'd mentioned the blue bottle first, so I figured that one was in the right position at the top of the triangle. So, with shaking fingers, I switched the yellow and the red bottles just as Vulnyx hooked his talons onto my arm.

"Aahh!" I screamed, recoiling in horror.

And at that moment, there came a sudden rush of rainbow light from the circle in the stones. The bottles glowed, their red, yellow, and blue lights sparkling like a kaleidoscope. Ione and Vulnyx ran from the light, screaming in horror.

And then I saw that the butterflies were free. Hundreds and hundreds of them fluttered around us, their wings every color of the rainbow. I realized then that they had been Ione's prisoners too. Deco, my father, and I stood staring in wonder. Then I broke the spell.

"Dad!" I cried, running toward my father. I threw my arms around him and hugged him tight. "Dad, I always knew you were alive!"

Epilogue

You're probably wondering if we ever made it out of the maze and away from Shadow Rock. I won't keep you in suspense any longer—we did, thanks to some incredibly lucky events. Maybe it was the positive energy of the bottles defeating the powers of evil. No scientist would agree with that, I know, but nothing about my experiences on the Islands of the Black Moon could be explained by science alone.

Anyway, the first lucky thing was that my father, Deco, and I were able to follow Deco's trail of X's back to the opening of the maze. Prepared to find the door locked, we were shocked to see that not only was it wide open, but it had been blown clear off its frame. Then the most amazing thing happened. Waiting for us, looking fit and healthy, stood not only the little white winged horse, but the entire herd, including the great white.

Each of us mounted a horse, and with my father leading the way, we flew to the Isle of Winds. There we freed all the scientists and doctors and teachers who were locked up in the dungeon where the manticores had imprisoned them so many years before. Deco picked the locks, of course.

Then we all set out for Bell Isle. As we descended, we heard the most beautiful music. Just listening to it made me shiver in delight.

"What is that music?" I called, peering downward.

"It's the bell!" cried Deco, pointing to the bell tower, which we could see in the moonlight as we neared the ground. "The silver bell is ringing!"

"Just like in the story," I gasped.

My father smiled at me as the horses descended toward the bell tower, where a huge crowd had gathered. Butterflies flitted through the air all around them, free at last from Ione's spell. The sultan came to greet us, with the old scientist from Tower Island just a few steps behind him. One of the winged horses had gone to fetch him. All around us people jostled, smiling and laughing, trying to get a look at us and the white winged horses.

"Welcome to Bell Isle!" called the sultan with a big smile, spreading his arms wide.

"Wow!" exclaimed Deco. "I guess the sultan ain't

under a spell anymore. I mean, he never talked to anybody before. And he never came outside and smiled and laughed and stuff."

The people all cheered the sultan as the soldiers raised their silver swords in salute.

"Are those soldiers the ones that used to be manticores?" I asked, staring at the smiling men, looking for a trace of their angry tiger faces and sharp pointy teeth.

"Guess so," said Deco.

I dismounted and stood next to him, my father right behind us.

"Thanks to you, the spell has been broken and our kingdom is whole again!" the sultan proclaimed. "Children have been reunited with their parents, and parents with their children. The bottles are back where they belong, and the evil Vulnyx and Ione have disappeared."

"Hooray!" all the people cheered.

I stole a glance at Deco, but he was looking the other way. I guess he really didn't have parents, because he sure wasn't trying to find them. He turned to me then with a big smile on his face, so I grinned back.

"And now I would like everyone to meet our new minister of science," said the sultan. The old man we had met in the tower stepped forward. "Once again, the people of Tower Island will devote themselves to the search for answers to the secrets of nature and to the invention of new and wonderful things."

The old scientist smiled and winked at me.

At a nudge from my father, I approached the sultan's jeweled throne and bowed. Then I turned to the old scientist and held out the lemon battery, its little yellow light glowing in my hand.

"You have brought a piece of the sun!" exclaimed the sultan in wonder.

"Actually, it's a lemon battery and it's powered by electricity," I said, winking at the old scientist. "I thought electricity might be something you'd like to discover next."

"Thank you," said the scientist, examining the lemon battery with one of his magnifying lenses.

"And you might as well take this, since it really belongs to you," I went on, handing him the telescope Ione had left behind in the maze.

"What is that tube?" asked the sultan, staring at the telescope like it was some strange creature.

"Look!" said the scientist, holding the telescope up to the sultan's eye and aiming it at one of the biggest stars in the dark night sky.

The sultan shouted in amazement. "This little girl has brought us a star!" he cried, and all the people cheered. Then he smiled at me. "You are quite an accomplished magician, little girl."

"You mean scientist," said the old scientist with another wink at me.

The sultan peered through the telescope again and

marveled some more over the lemon battery. "We will keep these precious things in a most sacred place, as befits the sun and the stars. Now, whatever you wish, it is my command."

"Thank you, Your Majesty," I said, bowing. "What we wish for is a boat so that we can sail home."

"Granted," boomed the sultan. "We have the boat in which your father journeyed here."

Everybody accompanied us down to the water's edge, where my father's boat was waiting. The next thing I knew, it was time to say good-bye to Deco.

"So long," I said, trying to swallow the lump that had suddenly risen in my throat. "I guess this is it."

"For now," said Deco, grinning his mischievous grin. "But I have a feeling I'm going to see you again."

"Well, thanks for everything," I blurted out, and then impulsively threw my arms around him.

"Lila!" called my dad from the boat. "It's time to go."

I hurried to the boat and waved good-bye to the crowd.

By the silver light of the black moon, we sailed until we came to the door in the air where my father had come through to this world. It was the same door that our ancestor Vasco da Gama, the great sea captain, had marked on his map. I hadn't noticed it because it looked like a blob in the middle of the ocean, unless, like my dad, you knew what it was supposed to be. Through the door shone light from another world . . . our world.

"Good-bye, Deco!" I whispered, turning to take one last look at the world of the Islands of the Black Moon.

As my father steered toward the opening in the air, I noticed a movement in the back of the boat. Something was wriggling its way out from under the canvas. Not some*thing*, I realized with a start, but some*one* with a blue cloth tied around his head and twinkling brown eyes. Deco!

But before I could say a word, the boat sailed through the magical door back to my world, and when I turned around, the door had disappeared into the night.